UNRAVELING

THE IMMUNE - BOOK 1

DAVID KAZZIE

GRUB CLUB PUBLISHING

COPYRIGHT

DEDICATION

As Always, For My Kids

ALSO BY DAVID KAZZIE

ACKNOWLEDGMENTS

To Dave Buckley, Matt Phillips, Wes Walker, Scott Weinstein, Kerry Wortzel, Rima Wiggin and others for their valuable input on early drafts of the manuscript.

To Geoffrey O'Neill and James Pickral for their insight on military matters.

To Hiba Mosrie, M.D., for her assistance with medical matters.

To Rachel at Littera Designs for her beautiful cover design work on the Four-Book Edition and Debbie at The Cover Collection for her amazing work on Unraveling, Void, Evergreen, and Citadel.

All errors are mine alone.

~

In the middle of the journey of our life I came to myself within a dark wood where the straight way was lost.

DANTE
THE DIVINE COMEDY

~

1

Miles Chadwick sat in a corner booth of Keens Steakhouse on West 36th Street in Manhattan, waiting for the apocalypse to begin.

A medium-rare filet mignon, accompanied by a side of fresh asparagus, sat in front of him, prepared to fulfill its destiny as his dinner. Chadwick stared absently at the food as if he wasn't quite sure what to do with it. He poked at the plump, crisp stalks of asparagus with his fork, their presentation on his plate reminding him of the gruesome black-and-white Holocaust photographs he'd seen as a schoolboy growing up in Carbondale, Illinois, of bodies stacked together like so much cordwood. That this was the memory flickering in his mind was ironic, given the course his life had taken, given the final answer to his own personal game of *What Do You Want to be When You Grow Up?*

As he sat there, considering this great irony, the smokiness of the charred meat began tickling his nose, which made him think of something even more horrific than the photographs, and it made his stomach flip a little. Because when you got right down to it, the thing he was now a party to was no different than the things he'd seen in those photographs. Had he really thought he was somehow better than that because he wasn't discriminating against this group or that one?

He took a deep breath and looked back at his filet. Maybe looking at it was nauseating him more than eating it would, and besides, he hadn't eaten anything all day, and so he ate every bite, chewing his meat slowly and thoroughly, just in case it might be his karmic comeuppance to choke to death on the day his plan was set into motion.

After cleaning his plate, even taking the time to wipe up the steak's juices with a crusty pumpernickel roll, he sipped his Dalwhinnie – four fingers' worth, because if there had ever been a time for scotch and a lot of it, it was now – and looked out across the wood-paneled dining room, which was packed to the gills tonight.

He first held his gaze on a group of young men in their mid-twenties at a table near the center of the main dining room, laughing like drunken hyenas. There was a wave of energy emanating from the table, a vibe that every one of these men would be getting a lap dance sometime in the next two hours. They were well-dressed and loud, commodities traders or investment bankers, managing the latter-day ritual of simultaneously yelling at one another and checking their smartphones. Empty beer and wine bottles littered the table like fallen soldiers on the pitch of battle, and reinforcements were on the way. If there was one thing Chadwick had learned about fine dining, it was that the amount of money a group spent on food and booze was directly proportional to the amount of noise it was allowed to make at dinner.

At the next table, two elderly couples, dressed for the theater. He couldn't quite make out what they were saying, but he would have bet all the money in his wallet that they were talking about tough times, how things used to be back during the Depression, discussions he hated listening to. Just hearing old people talk made his stomach muscles clench, what with their faux surprise at how fast everything was changing and how they never had anything to eat growing up other than soup rendered from the sweat of their shirts. He wondered what they would have thought about the truly hard times ahead, if any of them were fortunate enough (or unlucky enough, depending on your perspective) to survive. Probably won't be able to impress the young'uns with tales of the Depression and your black-and-white televisions, you old farts.

A third table, a booth just catty corner to him, was the hardest to look at. A man in his early forties, eating with his twin teenage sons. The man wore no wedding band, maybe Dad's weekend with the boys while his ex-wife got on with her life as a single mom. On the one hand, he pegged the father for a douchebag, dropping three hundred bucks on dinner when the boys would've been happy with a twelve-dollar bucket of chicken; on the other, the boys looked like they were having a ball, each of them chowing on porterhouses almost as big as they were. Difficult as it was, Chadwick made himself watch the boys eat their steaks, to make sure he didn't forget what they'd spent so many years working for.

Chadwick wondered if any of them would still be alive a month from now. Unlikely. Very unlikely. But he just didn't know what was going to happen. They had planned and planned and worked and worked, and there was no way to know how things would play out until they just went ahead and did it. There were about a hundred people in the restaurant that night. At least one of them would be naturally immune to the virus. Possibly two, but probably just one. He found himself hoping it would be one of the boys. He watched them dip their steak fries in ranch dressing and drink their cherry Cokes, and he watched their dad let them steal a nip from his tall glass of beer, painfully aware the trio would almost certainly be dead by Labor Day, four weeks from now.

Another wave of nausea washed over him, and he shut his eyes tight, trying to will away the queasiness. He'd known this was coming, and why in God's name he had just eaten a nine-ounce filet was beyond his powers of comprehension. Probably no one in human history had ever felt as much stress as what Miles Chadwick was feeling at this very moment. He gagged, fearful he had confused stomach-liquefying panic with hunger.

His phone began chirping, which just added fuel to his already overheated heart. One of the elderly foursome threw a nasty look in his direction, clearly unhappy with the technological intrusion. He resisted the nearly overpowering urge to flip her the bird, reminding himself that older folks still had a problem with the wireless phones in public, and besides, she'd be dead by the end of the week, so who cared what she thought?

The phone was a dinosaur, prepaid, purchased with cash at a 7-Eleven, for one use, for this moment only. At the other end of the line was another prepaid wireless phone, also purchased for this one historic telephone call. He struggled to grip the phone, which refused to find purchase in his sweat-slicked hand.

"Yes?" he answered, his voice catching.

Jesus, Chadwick, man up.

He cleared his throat, then more forcefully: "Yes?"

He could feel his heart pounding in his ears while he waited for a response.

"It's done."

"You're sure?" Chadwick asked.

"As sure as we're going to be right now. All canisters were deployed without issue or interference."

Reflexively, he touched his left bicep, the site of the vaccine administration one year ago. He would've bet anything that the caller had just done the same thing. Now they'd see if things unfolded as they predicted. Following exposure, an asymptomatic but contagious incubation period of about eight to twelve hours, which would facilitate the spread of the virus, and then another twelve to twenty-four hours for the disease to run its course. The key was the virus' design, Chadwick's engineering, its remarkable communicability and lethality.

"And there were no problems?"

"No problems," the man said. "All operatives reported in on schedule with the appropriate code word. Everything went according to plan. Fucking unbelievable, eh?"

Along with the very special vaccine to the soon-to-be-famous virus, relief coursed through Miles Chadwick's veins. But it wasn't just relief; riding shotgun was a sudden horror at what he had wrought. Part of him, and not a small one, wished he could undo what he had done, wished he had never created the PB-815 virus, impressionable and easily manipulated, like an insecure teenage girl, which he had brainwashed into becoming a ruthless serial killer. It was too much, too extreme, too fucking crazy. He felt cold; a shiver rippled through him.

"You still there?" the caller asked.

"Yes. Sorry."

He was biting his lip so hard that he had drawn blood. The taste of iron filled his mouth like he'd been chewing on a penny. He dabbed his lower lip with a napkin; he looked down at it, noticing that the tiny red spot left behind had taken the shape of a scythe. This he wrote off to his mind playing tricks on him. Still, he didn't want to keep looking at it, the non-symbolic symbol, so he quickly stuffed the napkin into his coat pocket. Scotch, he thought. The scotch would settle him down. He demolished the rest of his drink in one fell swoop.

"Now we wait, right?" the caller said.

"Now we wait," Chadwick confirmed. We wait, Chadwick thought, until nothing happens, or people start dying like flies. One or the other. "We'll meet at the compound in two weeks."

"Enjoy the rest of your summer," the caller said before clicking off the line.

That brought the faintest of smiles to Chadwick's

lips, and he immediately felt bad about it because it was disrespectful, making jokes at the expense of the human race.

Chadwick ordered a second scotch and glanced at the boys, each now laying waste to a slice of chocolate pie. Then he turned his attention to the front door, positive that any minute now, a hundred federal agents would swarm in like locusts and arrest him, giving the restaurant's other patrons the winning story at their next get-together. They would charge him with about fifty different violations of the federal antiterrorism statute, and he'd have an all-expense paid trip to the execution chamber at the supermax prison in Florence, Colorado. Wasn't that how it always played out in the movies? The bad guy never got away. Didn't the hero always crack the case at the last minute, saving everyone at the zero hour?

Every shred of doubt about his intellect or ability that he had ever felt in his life drew up into a tsunami of fear and panic and washed through him like a flash flood hitting a barren gulley. How could he have been so stupid, so arrogant, so foolish? Who was he to think that he could alter the course of human history? He thought about all he was trying to undo, thousands of years of human achievement, from the wheel to the computer, from fried Twinkies to bluegrass music, from Harley-Davidson to the moon landing. His plan was too big, too insane, too impossible.

He took another sip of scotch, a long one. Calm down, he whispered to himself. Calm down. He closed his eyes and counted to twenty. Finally, finally, the alcohol started to work its magic, and he felt warmth at his core, spreading out to his extremities, his face, and at long last, his brain. His mind settled, he thought about the plan again, a decade in the making. Its genesis, its infancy, its rocky adolescence, and finally, tonight's debut. He reached into his pocket and pulled out the photograph he'd carried for two decades. Ragged on the edges, folded and unfolded so many times that the creases had split. He stared at the picture, and it reminded him why he was doing this, why he'd made it his life's work to make PB-815 all that it could be.

A basic tenet of virology was that viruses could be extremely lethal or extremely communicable, but not both. Thus, a quick-killing virus, the type that became fodder for movies and books and scaring the bejeezus out of people, normally faced one of two fates: either it burned itself out and disappeared because it killed its host too rapidly, before it had a chance to jump to the next one, or it mutated into a less virulent form to ensure the hosts stayed alive long enough to perpetuate the virus' continued survival. See, e.g., the common cold, which ran unchecked around the globe, a big, dumb, happy germ that just wanted everyone to like it. The Labrador retriever of the virus world.

Chadwick believed there was a reason that the Ebolas of the world had stayed put, occasionally rearing their heads to remind humanity that they were still here, but never quite making the big crash into the human race. At their core, these super-hot viruses, like Ebola and Marburg, were programmed to stay hot, and so the price they paid for their deadliness was existence on the fringe. They were viral royalty, not interested in infecting millions or billions at the risk of sacrificing their virulence, satisfied, maybe at some unknowable level, at being the very best with a limited body of work.

But then Chadwick had created PB-815 while working for that private, off-the-books laboratory in southern Nebraska, funded by Leon Gruber, the benefactor who had started the project. Without government oversight to worry about, Chadwick's work progressed quickly. Within two years, he'd developed his masterpiece – a jacked-up virus with the serial-killer drive of Ebola and spliced with the sociability of the commonest of colds. He was fortunate the virus hadn't claimed him along the way. But their tedious, careful, painstaking work had been completed, not just on the virus, but on the vaccine as well, because without the vaccine, a true marvel, PB-815 was useless, a monster that couldn't be controlled, a beast that would turn on its handlers.

And now it was ready. If everything went according

to plan, it would spread quickly, so quickly that if the virus indeed did mutate a few weeks from now, it wouldn't matter. Chadwick had made his peace with the fact that there were certain things beyond his control, that no one truly knew how PB-815 would interact with a complex system like the vast tapestry making up the human population. In fact, a very tiny fraction of the population, perhaps less than two percent, would be naturally immune to the virus thanks to a genetic anomaly he'd discovered. Boy, were those folks in for a big surprise.

They had estimated the first wave of infections at about five thousand, five thousand people who would leave tonight's Yankees game with a very special souvenir, and each of whom would infect a dozen or so people before becoming symptomatic themselves, about eight to twelve hours after exposure. Before the first wave began dying about a day from now, they would have spread the virus to about another 60,000 people. Then their virus would truly go viral, up to five million before health officials even got wind of an outbreak, and then that, as they said, would be all she wrote. And he wasn't even counting the supercarriers, the ones who would board airplanes and buses and trains and subways and expose hundreds, if not thousands, of people in one fell swoop, and send the virus to the four points of the compass, aboard the transatlantic flights to London and Paris and Johannesburg, the westbound airliners to Tokyo and Sydney and Beijing, on the morning shuttles to Chicago and Washington and Los Angeles and Houston, cutting any effective quarantine attempts off at the legs.

Miles Chadwick held up his tumbler of scotch and silently toasted the noisy dining room, a eulogy for a world that had ended at Yankee Stadium, during the second of a three-game series between the Bombers and the Red Sox, the teams tied for first place with eight weeks to go in the regular season, the baseball universe in its proper order.

2

Adam Fisher held the letter in his hands, the words lying flat against the page. Standing alone, each word was just that – a word, meaningless without context, a dictionary entry. But strung together in this way, on this sheet of paper bearing the letterhead of the Virginia Board of Medicine, the words joined together into something accusatory, something lethal, something ruinous. He read it again, skimming over the clutter and procedure of the opening paragraph and focusing on the meat, a single sentence near the bottom of the heavy bond paper the Board used in flexing its muscles when summoning its licensees before it.

Specifically, Adam Fisher, M.D., failed to adequately monitor Patient A, who was 39 weeks pregnant, causing the patient's death and the loss of the full-term fetus.

Twenty-six words. Twenty-six words that had chewed their way into the fabric of his life like moths set loose in a musty closet. Twenty-seven, if you counted the M.D., the two letters that meant so much to so many people, the two letters that earned him a spot in Richmond Magazine's list of Most Eligible Bachelors every couple of years, the two letters that had placed him under the jurisdiction of the Board of Medicine since he'd become licensed as a physician sixteen years earlier.

He set the letter down on his blotter and leaned back in his chair. He was in his private office at the Tuckahoe Women's Center, on the campus of the Henrico Doctors' Hospital, a few miles west of downtown Richmond, Virginia. It was early, a little after seven, and the office was still quiet. The day promised a full slate of expectant mommies, menopausal grandmothers, teenage girls embarrassed by their mothers hell-bent on getting them on birth control. Adam hadn't slept since the letter from the Board had arrived in yesterday's mail. Of course, he'd known it was coming since that awful day the previous November. It was like waiting eight months for a punch in the stomach, a punch you knew was going to drop you and take your breath away, but one that you couldn't do anything about.

His gaze drifted up to the large corkboard pinned to his wall, every square inch covered with photographs, the faces of countless babies staring back at him, children he'd shepherded into the world. He'd never planned to start the Baby Board, as it was known in the office, but early in his career, following a patient's difficult but successful delivery, the new mom had sent him a photo of her healthy baby. Not knowing what to do with it, Adam pinned it to the new corkboard, an office accoutrement he hadn't found a use for yet. A week later, another patient saw the picture during her last office visit before delivery, and she too sent a photograph of her newborn. And it grew from there. Not every patient sent in a picture, but many did, and in sixteen years, the board had filled up, getting more and more crowded until it looked like a giant group shot of a baby rave.

Adam started each day with a quick look at his body of work, at the chubby babies, the skinny ones, preemies, late arrivals, the Down Syndrome babies, the healthy babies, black babies, white babies, Asian babies, Latino babies. The oldest, the very first picture on the bulletin board, was in high school now; the newest photo was of a little boy born about three weeks ago. Two of the babies on the wall had since died, one of leukemia at the age of nine, the other in a car accident before her first birthday. Neither mother was his patient anymore; Adam didn't know if it was appropriate to keep those photos up, but he couldn't bear to take them down, and so there they remained.

He thought about Patient A again, who'd said at her last appointment that she couldn't wait to send in her picture for the board.

At 7:45, he changed into a spare pair of khakis and button-down oxford he kept at the office and eyed the worn couch in the corner, a holdover from the old apartment he'd lived in during med school. He'd been up for twenty-four hours, but Adam had never needed much sleep, a useful skill for a doctor. It would be more for the brief escape from this new reality of his. He rubbed his eyes, ran his hands against his closely shorn hair, decided against the nap. He sat back down and read the letter again. For the hundredth time? The thousandth? He didn't know.

A knock on his open office door interrupted him, and he felt a burst of heat run up his back, as if someone had caught him looking at Internet porn. He briefly debated stuffing the letter in his desk, but then it would look like he was trying to cover what he was doing, and then it would look like he was admitting he was guilty of the terrible thing the letter was accusing him of, that he had, in fact, failed to adequately monitor Patient A, which, of course, was a euphemism for *killing* Patient A and her unborn baby, who had been doing just fine, thank you very much, until Dr. Adam Fisher had gotten his incompetent hands on them.

During a professional ethics class he'd taken his

last year in medical school, one of those weekly classes he frequently skipped, Adam had been required to observe a hearing before the Board of Medicine. It was a *Scared Straight* sort of thing, designed to remind these fledgling doctors that they should avoid the Board offices, unless they'd made the right kind of friends and gotten themselves appointed to the Board itself. Adam couldn't even remember what the respondent, an oncologist (or was it a cardiologist?), had been charged with. He'd gotten there late, a little hungover, and could barely manage to stay awake during the interminable hearing. He remembered very clearly thinking that would never happen to him, feeling a certain detached pity for this poor sap before the Board, four doctors and one chiropractor (a chiropractor – for God's sake, medicine's equivalent of a snake oil salesman!) second-guessing his life's work.

He looked up and saw Joe McCann standing in the doorway. He was a large man, and despite having rounded the turn toward his seventieth birthday, he was still blessed with a shock of thick red hair topping his huge dome. This was his medical practice, now in its fourth decade of serving the Richmond area. He didn't work a full schedule anymore, but he still had his finger on the pulse of what his six physicians were up to.

"Morning," Adam said. He didn't try to put on airs or pretend like nothing was wrong, because Joe would have sniffed it out in a heartbeat. Worse, he would have felt like his intelligence was being insulted, and there was nothing the man hated more.

"How you doing, son?" McCann asked.

So he knew. Of course he knew. Did Adam really think he wouldn't know? McCann had friends everywhere in the medical community, including, but not limited to the Virginia Board of Medicine. Besides, there was nothing secret about the Board's Notice for Adam L. Fisher, M.D., to appear on September 9, some five weeks hence. It was public record, out there for all eternity, so even if Adam was fully exonerated, that Notice would be out there for all to see, a little whisper in the ear of a prospective patient who'd decided to check Adam out, telling her the terrible story of Patient A.

Adam was a little relieved McCann knew. It was out of the way, and Adam was spared the humiliation of having to knock on McCann's door like a kid who'd smashed his neighbor's window with an errant baseball.

Adam took a deep breath and let it out slowly.

"I've been better," Adam said.

"I know, son," McCann said. He addressed each of his three male doctors as son. "We'll get through this. It's a bullshit charge, but you can't let it eat you up like this."

"I'll be OK," Adam said. "The work will keep my

mind off it. We're loaded up with Amanda on maternity leave."

McCann closed the door and dropped his big frame down on Adam's couch. He leaned forward, propping his elbows on his knees.

"Here's the thing," McCann said. "I've been thinking about this a lot. I want you to take a little time off so you can deal with this thing. Get your head straight. I have every confidence the Board will clear you, but you're no good to me while you replay every moment of that night every minute of the day."

Adam looked at his boss, his mouth agape.

"Are you firing me?" Adam asked, his voice small. The office felt hot all of a sudden.

"No," McCann said. "Absolutely not. I'll pay your salary until the hearing, and then they'll reprimand you or cut you loose or whatever it is they're going to do, and we can all move on with our lives. Look, I've read the chart. I talked to the nurses on duty. You did every goddamn thing I would've done. Sometimes patients die."

Adam couldn't hold McCann's gaze; he fiddled with the blotter, his fingers peeling up the corner of the August calendar.

"I don't know. I just don't know."

"I've been watching you the last few months," McCann said. "You second-guess yourself. You order unnecessary tests. You scare patients. You're like

Chicken Little all of a sudden. You're a good doctor, a goddamn good doctor, but this is no good for you, no good for the patients. Adam. Sometimes they just die."

Adam wanted to argue, shout, beg, plead, bargain, do something, anything to keep working. He dreaded the idea of five empty weeks ahead of him, nothing left to fill the time but his thoughts. But he remained silent. Once Joseph McCann had made up his mind about something, he didn't change it.

"What am I supposed to do for five weeks?"

McCann smiled.

"Whatever you want. Go to Vegas. Go visit your daughter."

The mention of Rachel made his stomach tighten. She was a rising sophomore at CalTech and lived with her mom Nina and stepfather Jerry near San Diego; Adam saw her once or twice a year. He couldn't bear to tell her about this. Their relationship had finally reached a point where they spoke regularly, where he didn't feel like an interloper in her life. This though, he was afraid how she would see him in her eyes. She would see herself in Patient A. She would see her mom, her closest friends, because that's how she thought, how her mind worked. And she would think less of him. This just served to depress him further. Just tack on *Shitty Doctor* alongside his talent as *Absent Father*!

McCann pointed at the letter on Adam's desk.

Before continuing, he grimaced and struggled to clear his throat. He coughed twice.

"Are you OK?" Adam asked.

"Yeah," McCann said. "Woke up feeling a little off. Might be coming down with something." He felt around under his neck. "Glands are a bit swollen."

"I can stay and work today," Adam offered. "You wanna go home?"

"Fisher, if I went home every time I felt a little under the weather, I wouldn't be much of a doctor, now would I?" McCann asked.

"You're not gonna let me slide on this little vacation, are you?"

McCann winked at him.

"Good one." He rapped twice on the doorjamb before disappearing down the hall, calling back as he ducked into his own office.

"Work on getting that thing out of your life."

HE DROVE HOME SLOWLY, sticking to the city streets, thick with rush-hour traffic headed toward downtown Richmond for another workday under the broiling August sun. This time of year, the traffic was made up of two groups of people - those who'd already been on vacation and were already missing it, and those who'd yet to escape on their summer getaway. Adam turned south on Robinson, rolled by Buddy's Bar & Grill, one of his old med school hangouts, when life had been so much easier. His whole career ahead of him.

Traffic slowed at Robinson and West Grace Street, and Adam coasted to a halt. The oscillating lights of emergency vehicles in the intersection flickered silently in the morning steam. Two paramedics worked to load a stretcher into the ambulance bay, and a police officer directed traffic down a side street. In the middle of the intersection, the mangled remains of a motor-cycle and the spider-webbed windshield of a Ford Taurus, parked at a crazy angle.

Adam rolled down his window as he approached the officer. He was stoutly built, his beefy arms straining against the short-sleeve police uniform.

"I'm a doctor," Adam said to the man. "Need any help?"

"Naw, thanks," the officer said. "Car versus motor-cycle. Dumbass wasn't wearing a helmet. DOA."

Adam sighed. Callous as his words might have been, the officer was correct that the biker had been a dumbass.

"Sorry to hear it," Adam said.

"Thanks anyway, doc."

Another block south, he turned right onto Floyd Avenue and found a spot just in front of his two-story brownstone. The premier parking spot was, to Adam, a pretty shitty attempt at evening the cosmic scales.

Yeah, yeah, so your career is on the line and you just drove by a fatal car crash, but how about that primo parking spot, big A! Still, if that was all that the universe was prepared to offer him today, then he would take it. Maybe, just maybe, this good parking spot was the bloop single triggering a long streak of good fortune.

He checked the mail and made his way up the front walk, past his small yard, roasted to a burnt orange, the product of another hot, dry, merciless summer in central Virginia. Maybe the planet was warming, and maybe they were all roasting themselves one barrel of oil at a time. Or maybe it was because the world was such an angry place these days, and a hot, angry planet was just what mankind deserved.

He'd bought the place just after finishing medical school, when he learned he'd been matched with the Virginia Commonwealth University Hospital in downtown Richmond for his OB/GYN residency. After a childhood spent in Culpeper County, a rural stretch of horse farms and not much else in central Virginia, he'd grown to love city living, in no small part because his father Donald, an accomplished computer scientist and giant prick, hated it so much. His house was in a historical neighborhood of brownstones and Victorian-style mansions called the Fan, so named because of how its half dozen or so main streets fanned out from a centerpoint near the VCU campus.

He liked its feel, of sitting on his porch and drinking a cold Sam Adams when he wasn't on call, smoking the occasional cigarette (even though he was a doctor and, of course, he knew better). In the evenings, he liked walking around the corner to Pints & Pies and eating pizza while listening to the local music scene. Sometimes, he'd make the acquaintance of a young lady, and that would last a few weeks or a few months, long enough to make him realize she wasn't The One either. He liked his strange hippie neighbors, the poet on his left, the alternative fuels guy on his right.

As he let himself in, he took note of how quiet it was. He wasn't here often on weekday mornings, and so he wasn't especially tuned in to the neighborhood's weekday rhythms. The whole neighborhood was ghost-like, a shadow of its normal self. He didn't see any joggers or stay-at-home moms pushing their strollers like he expected. It unnerved him a little. Quiet mornings in the beach cottage, those were different, when the lines on the calendar dissolved. The silence spurred him on, urging him to pack quickly.

He threw clothes and toiletries into an overnight bag. A stack of unread novels stood precariously on his nightstand, books he'd collected during his trips to the various local bookstores, and he imagined himself sitting at the water's edge lost in a long book, his feet buried in the wet, shifting sand. There was something

about a long novel that Adam had always found allur-
ing, the way he could disappear into the story and not
look up until the tops of his thighs had burned to a
crisp. A couple of paperbacks found their way into his
bag as well. After packing, he hopped online and
suspended his mail service, his newspaper, set up his
bills to auto-pay.

Adam leaned back in his chair and scratched his
chin, sandpapery with a couple of days of stubble. He
thought about calling Rachel, who would be getting
ready to head back to campus. He took out his phone
and dialed her number, his heart throbbing. As it rang
unrequitedly, he wondered, like he always did when he
called and no one answered, if she was sitting there in
Sunnydale, holding the phone in her hand as his name
flashed on the caller ID, deciding whether she should
answer the phone.

He was greeted by the phone's prerecorded
message, which always made him smile; he once asked
her why she didn't leave her own outgoing message on
her phone, and she'd said she didn't have time to waste
on bullshit like that. Bullshit, she'd said. That was
Rachel.

"Hey, Rach," he began, "it's Dad."

He paused, trying to think of something funny to
say, but as the seconds ticked by, he became aware of
the silence, of the hiss of the open phone line, and how
the silence would sound on her end.

"Sorry about that," he said. "Dropped an apple." His cheeks flushed with embarrassment. "Anyway, I'm headed out down to the beach house for a little vacation. I know you're probably busy getting ready for school, but I'd love to hear from you. Give me a call when you get a chance. Bye."

He nearly told her he loved her but decided against it. He hung up.

He started to get out of his chair, but then he sat back down and pulled up the website of an online florist. Daffodils had always been her favorite, and as sensible as she was, she'd always had a soft spot for flowers. He found an arrangement he thought she would like, cursed at the outrageous price - really, seventy-nine bucks for eight flowers and a cheap glass vase? He raced through the order, pausing at the screen asking for a personalized message.

Rach,

I know you'll do great this year.

Love,

Dad

He left it at that.

ADAM LEFT Richmond a little after noon. It was about a five-hour trip, taking him south-southeast through tobacco country for about 175 miles before doglegging east toward Wilmington on Interstate 40. It rained lightly, off and on for most of the first half of the drive. Adam passed the time by imagining where each driver was headed.

He stopped once, just east of the I-95/I-40 junction, for fuel and a gas station hot dog, a guilty pleasure he admitted to no one. He ate in the shade of the pump island as the nozzle delivered its payload into his gas tank. The concrete shimmered in the heat, cooking the scraggly weeds poking up through the zig-zaggy cracks here and there across the tarmac. A tired-looking banner strung across the building's façade announced the sale of a $50,000 SuperLotto ticket, and Adam wondered about the type of person who would be swayed to buy a lottery ticket by the display of such an advertisement. The crumpled-up remains of his lunch flew into the wastebasket, he imagined himself burying a three-pointer to bring the Wizards their first NBA title since the 1970s, and he got back on the road.

It was murderously humid, the sky a hard blue, the kind of day that would fire up big thunderheads by dinnertime, scaring the beachgoers off the sand and into their cottages and condos, the ones with any sense anyway. Even on full blast, the air conditioning strained to keep the car cool, and he grew impatient, the little boy in him wondering when the hell they were going to get there already. Traffic was relatively light as he made his way southeast. The southern

North Carolina beaches were still a relatively well-kept secret, and the easy access always made for a relaxing start to a vacation.

A little after five, he turned east off Route 17 and rolled past the vegetable stands and crumbling postwar ranch houses toward the coast. A few minutes later, the white causeway leading to the skinny island of Holden Beach arced up in Adam's windshield. To the west, the sky had darkened, a line of purplish clouds with mayhem on the brain. They looked like a giant bruise on the sky, a harbinger of atmospheric violence to come.

He stopped for groceries and supplies at the big store just before the causeway. Might as well get it out of the way, he thought. He bought steaks, chicken, ribs, sausage; he scoured the less-than-impressive produce aisle because after all that meat, he'd need something to keep the plumbing clear, he stocked up on chips and cookies and beer. As he made his way up and down the aisles, grabbing batteries and pancake mix and bacon, magical, delicious bacon, and whatever else his heart desired, his body loosened, his mind decelerated.

His Explorer stocked with groceries, Adam climbed the causeway slowly, taking in the Atlantic Ocean ahead, gray and choppy on this summer afternoon. Humid air wafted through the open windows, the salty brine tickling his nose. He could hear the waves, the sound of the ocean, of this monolithic thing, forever there, and he could feel his blood pressure drop. Once he was on the island, he picked his way past the quaint post office, past the sign announcing TURTLE PATROL THURSDAY NIGHT 7 PM! before turning west along Ocean Boulevard.

Since it was a weekday, not a turnaround day, the traffic was light on the island's main drag, and he covered the remaining miles to his cottage in the blink of an eye. He was careful not to speed, though, because if there was anything the Brunswick County Sheriff's deputies loved doing, it was ticketing speeders, folks who would never come back to contest the charge six weeks later, long after the vacation had ended and they were knee deep in the routine of their everyday lives.

THE HOUSE WAS one of the older ones, a gray, weather-beaten A-frame, right on the beach, built in the 1960s by Adam's grandfather, Jack Fisher, plank by plank. He had died when Adam was five, leaving the house to Adam's father. And because Don Fisher was nothing if not thrifty, Adam had spent many summer vacations and spring breaks and Christmases here as a kid, so many that he began to resent the place, because would it have killed his dad to take him to Disney World or Hawaii or California just one time? Donald Fisher was a difficult man who'd never recovered from the sudden death of Adam's mother, and he used the house as a drinking oasis, a place for him to escape the disappointment that was his life. He brought Adam here because he could let him run on the beach while he sat in a rickety old rocking chair on the deck, drinking can after can of Pabst Blue Ribbon.

As he got older, Adam grew to appreciate Holden more, and when he got his driver's license, he started coming down here on his own and taking care of the place, which was fine by the senior Fisher. Adam taught himself some simple renovations, looked to the neighbors for help when he got stuck on something, and slowly but surely made the place a wellspring of happy memories rather than a cesspool of sour ones.

After turning on the water main at the front of the house and a quick exterior inspection, Adam let himself in, finding the house to be in relatively good shape, if not a little musty. He went from room to room, checking window seals, looking for yellow stains in the ceiling, the telltale sign of water damage, finding none. A few bulbs had burned out since he'd last been here, but otherwise, the place just needed a good airing out.

It took three trips to unload the Explorer, but an hour later, the truck was empty, the supply closet and the pantry fully stocked. The approaching thunderheads had dissolved, leaving behind a checkered sky of clouds and sun. Adam stretched out on one of the weather-beaten Adirondack chairs on the back deck, looking out over the ocean, a cold beer in his hand, a portable cooler stocked with a six-pack next to him. He'd brought a paperback out here with him, the latest Dennis Lehane, but he was content to watch the ocean and the sunbathers dotting the beach like brightly colored hermit crabs scampering across the sand.

He stayed out on the deck all evening, drinking his beer, slapping at the lazy mosquitoes droning around him. For the first time in nearly a year, Patient A seemed very far away.

3

"It's over, Freddie," Richie Matas said. "You understand what I'm saying, right?"

Freddie Briggs was seated on the ridiculous rattan couch in their sunroom, barely aware of his wife Susan's hand at his back, caressing him, trying to calm him down. The room was bright with sunlight, streaming in from the huge plate-glass windows.

"No one will touch you after the positive test," said Richie, his longtime agent, a founding partner of Elite Sports Worldwide and the one who'd been lucky enough to snag Freddie as he was coming out of college a decade ago. "It's over."

Richie paused and then said it again, like a mob hitman putting another bullet in his victim's head to make sure the job had been done. Then Freddie was up off the couch, prowling like a mountain lion, a scary enough vibe emanating from him to encourage his ever-pacing agent to take a seat next to Susan.

"Freddie," Susan was saying, "it's gonna be OK. We're gonna figure this out."

"Didn't I tell you to stay away from that shit?" Richie asked. "They got tests we can't keep up with. Did you know **you** what it was when you took it? We'll file an appeal."

Freddie ignored him, not wanting to discuss it in front of Susan, even though he knew she knew about it. It was one of those things shared between a husband and wife without being shared, disapproved of in non-verbal ways. She hadn't asked about the hypodermic needle or the vial because as any good lawyer would tell you, you never asked the question you didn't want the answer to. Freddie, his hands clenching into fists and unclenching again, peered out the plate-glass window overlooking the backyard, sloping down toward the lake about a hundred yards distant. To the right was Susan's vegetable garden, in full bloom now, exploding in reds and greens and yellows. Beyond that, the acre of land made possible by an NFL career that appeared to have reached its end.

"Those assholes. Those assholes!"

He never thought he'd be the guy to get busted, but there he was, thirty-two years old, trying to make it back from his second reconstructive knee surgery (on the same knee, no less) in three years. He wanted to tell Richie and Susan that the trainer he'd hooked up with in February had told him that they *didn't* test for that substance, which helped him recover from work-outs faster, but the truth was that the guy had said that they couldn't test for it. And Freddie just wanted to believe him so badly because the only thing that was going to get him another chance with the league was to make his body as hard and fast and strong as it had ever been. Then they'd pulled him for a random urine screen two weeks ago, just before the camps were about to open, just before he expected to get a call from Richie telling him that it was going to be Chicago or Houston or maybe New York that wanted to bring in the great Freddie Briggs to shore up a defensive line.

And Matas had called, this morning, in fact, saying he was in Smyrna meeting a potential client and that they needed to talk. When he got to the house, there was no indication that there was anything wrong even though he was pacing because he was always pacing. No clue he was planning to tell his most famous client the news he didn't want to hear, the professional athlete's equivalent of finding out the mass was malig-nant and that there wasn't anything else that could be done.

Freddie picked up an empty rattan chair and swung it around like an Olympic hammer before launching it through the sliding door. The door exploded like a starburst, shards and splinters of glass blowing out onto the composite deck.

"Freddie!"

He left them there, the sunroom silent but for the tinkling of the broken glass, back through the galley kitchen, the office, and through the family room, past his girls Caroline and Heather, sitting on the couch, watching *Tangled*, oblivious to what was going on around them in that way that kids were. He stopped at the front door, his hand on the knob, and debated just sitting with them as they watched their movie, but he couldn't. He couldn't breathe in here.

He climbed into his truck and drove off. He rolled past the huge homes in the subdivision, occupied by doctors and bankers who were good enough neighbors and had long ago gotten used to the idea of the NFL star next door. He wasn't sure where he was going, only sure that he couldn't be inside his house anymore, in front of Richie, in front of Susan, who would be so disappointed in him for cheating because she told him many years ago that she hoped he never thought he would need to do that.

Near the center of town, he turned down Walker Street and into the gravel parking lot of The Ugly Duckling, wedging his mammoth SUV next to a Ford F-150 with the naked-lady mudflaps, super close, almost hoping its owner would give him a hard time for parking so close to his beloved pickup, because it had been a while since Freddie had been in a good fight.

Freddie stamped across the dusty gravel parking lot and burst through the front door, feeling every bit the cliché of a man seeking to drown his sorrows in drink. His size and presence always drew stares, even from people who'd known him for years. He strode up to the long oak bar and asked Sal, the proprietor, for the Wild Turkey. Sal, who had known Freddie since he started patronizing the bar in high school, when he was already bigger, faster, and stronger than every man in Smyrna and could hold his booze better than the gin-blossomest drunk in the place, poured the shot without comment and left the bottle at Freddie's side.

Freddie drained two shots without blinking an eye, thinking back to his first day at the NFL scouting combines, when he'd left the scouts gasping for air with his 40-yard-dash time. It was legendary, adding to the ever-growing mythos of Freddie Briggs, the greatest defensive lineman in a generation.

He glanced around the bar before knocking back his third shot, still feeling like that teenager who'd snuck in here, too young to drink, even though he was a grown man now, married, father of two girls. The Ugly Duckling had been a Smyrna institution since opening its doors in 1985, making its home in the low-slung building with the giant plastic chick on the roof, keeping its little ducky eye on the town. Someone tried stealing it at least once a year.

As was often the case at happy hour, the bar was crowded with regulars, and people normally left him alone, especially lately, with his recent struggles documented in the Atlanta Journal-Constitution. This he had never quite gotten used to, and he wondered how regular people would react if their performance and career struggles were publicly documented on a regular basis.

Struggle. Something unimaginable three years ago, but rapidly becoming part of his everyday, part of his routine. Someone was telling him he couldn't do something, and there was nothing he could do about it. For all his physical gifts, for all his intellect, a combination of brains and brawn that made NFL scouts drool starting his freshman year at LSU and led some sports commentators to call him the next step in human evolution, it was his body that had finally failed him, leaving him washed up at thirty-two.

Six straight years he had made the Pro Bowl, the unquestioned captain and coach of the Atlanta Falcons defense, no matter who bore the title of defensive coordinator. Then on the first Sunday of his seventh season, rushing the Arizona Cardinals quarterback on a sellout blitz, the slow and overmatched left tackle had lost his balance and rolled into Freddie's right knee, planted firmly into the turf, tearing three ligaments and ripping the meniscus clean off. A year of rehabilitation followed, but he'd lost a step, probably more like three steps, in his return season. He blew out the knee again in the year's last game, and that was the end of that. The Falcons cut him, brutally and unceremoniously, a Hall of Fame career now in question. After another year of rehab, he signed on with New England as a backup lineman, but the knee wouldn't cooperate, and the Patriots cut him as well.

It was early August now, training camps in full swing, and he'd spent the last six months in the weight room, running five miles each day, desperate for one more chance to prove he was as good now as he had been during those six magical seasons with the Falcons. He had the skills, the veteran wiliness, and while he wasn't twenty-two anymore, a body that was more than up for the task. But now this positive test, and the four-game suspension that would follow had all but ended his career at the ripe old age of thirty-two. He wondered if it had hit ESPN or Yahoo! Sports yet; if not, it would soon, and then they would call him a cheater. The pride of Smyrna, nothing but a cheater.

He threw back the next shot, his head telling him he should stop now and scoot back home, where Richie and Susan were undoubtedly huddled together, trying to come up with a plan to soften the landing, make him understand that his football days had been numbered from the moment he'd pulled on a jersey for the Smyrna SkyChiefs in the pee-wee league he'd run roughshod over to the point that the other parents demanded to see a birth certificate because no way was that kid five years old. They would tell him a pro football career had a half-life, that there was life after football and he should be thankful he was leaving the game with nothing worse than a couple of bum knees.

He took a deep breath, slightly buzzed now, fully aware of the cliché he'd become – the ex-jock unable to let go of his glory, marinating his sorrows at the local watering hole. The reality was he didn't even need to be here to get drunk; he had a fully stocked bar in their media room, where he'd studied game film. But he couldn't be at the house anymore. Just being inside its walls was suffocating him, as if the oxygen had been sucked clean out of the house.

Freddie became aware of a presence beside him, another bar patron perched atop the cracked vinyl covering the ancient barstool, rotated just so, his right elbow propped up on the bar. From the corner of his eye, Briggs took in his new neighbor, and his heart sank. It was just not going to be his day.

It was Randy Ferguson, Campbell High School's ex-assistant football coach. He'd lost his job a year ago, after he'd been found in the back of his van with a cigar box full of weed and a fifteen-year-old cheerleader in an inappropriate stage of undress. Ferguson had been another one of Smyrna's shining football stars, not the wunderkind Briggs had been, but Division I material nonetheless, an outside chance to make it to the NFL as an offensive lineman. That dream had ended when he'd fractured two vertebrae in his neck during his sophomore season at Alabama, and Ferguson had never quite made his peace with that.

His hand was wrapped around a bottle of Coors Light, sweating condensation, the droplets catching the light from the bar just so. He was taller than Briggs and heavier, although Ferguson's current mass owed more to beer, pizza and cheese fries. Over the years, he'd developed a reputation as a bit of a brawler, but the fights always went one of two ways; he either knocked his opponent down with one swipe of his meaty mitt, or the brawls degenerated into a slow dance to nowhere.

"So, Freddie," Ferguson said, "how's the comeback going?"

Freddie rubbed his eye slowly, cursing his luck. If there had been a list of *Fucking People He Didn't Feel Like Dealing With*, Randy Ferguson would have been near the top of it. And he'd have to just sit here and take it because getting up and walking out would be just what Randy Ferguson would want; it would signify that Ferguson had won some battle in the eternal war between the two men, a war waged exclusively in Ferguson's head. Freddie and Ferguson had passed each other on the ladder to success, and Ferguson had never forgotten it.

"Fine," Freddie said. He poured another shot and threw it back.

"Been seeing you out running," Ferguson said. "Yeah, putting in the miles. But lemme ask you this – ain't training camps already started?"

Ferguson was drunk, talking loudly, his cheeks flushed, and his southern accent even more pronounced than usual. The volume was due in part to the booze, but it was intentional on a certain level, because Ferguson wanted nothing more than for Briggs to crash and burn, for his star to burn out, and he wouldn't have to hear about Freddie Briggs anymore.

Another shot. Freddie's head started to swim a little bit. He hadn't touched alcohol in six months, and it was hitting him harder and faster than he'd expected. He took a deep breath and let it out slowly, scanning the crowd in the mirror mounted behind the rows of bottles standing a vigilant watch. Every single person was watching the confrontation unfolding in front of them; all knew there was no love lost between the two local legends.

"You know they've started," Freddie said. No point in dancing around the issue. Maybe he'd take the wind out of Ferguson's sails, and the loser could get back to drinking himself to death or selling meth to underage girls or whatever it was he did all day.

"But I thought this was the big comeback year," Ferguson said, his observation coated with ice and snark. "Hometown hero makes good!"

"Go fuck yourself," Freddie said, his own voice booming. He poured another shot and held the glass up to Ferguson. "Cheers."

"Go fuck yourself?" he repeated.

Ferguson spun around to face the crowd, his beefy arms spread out theatrically; beer sloshed over the lip of his glass, splashing Freddie's arm.

"Everyone hear that?" Ferguson said. "Smyrna's golden boy has forgotten his manners!"

He turned back to face Freddie, close enough for Freddie to feel Ferguson's beer-soaked breath breaking across his face like a fetid tropical wind.

"Is that it?" Ferguson asked. "Have you forgotten your manners?"

"Not today, Randy," Freddie said, turning back away from his tormentor.

"Oh, I think today is a perfect day for it," Ferguson said, poking two meaty fingers into Freddie's shoulder. "A perfect day to teach you some fuckin' manners."

Freddie refused to look at the man, focusing his gaze on the beer taps in front of him, trying to ignore the growing heat in his belly.

"You listening to me, fuckstick?" Randy said,

another poke in Freddie's shoulder, this one more forceful. "Or are you Hall-of-Fame types too good for us regular folk?"

Freddie's right hand, palm open, exploded into Ferguson's sternum, knocking the drunk man off balance. Ferguson toppled over and hit the floor with a huge crash; the floor shook like a minor earthquake had hit the place.

The big man climbed back to his feet, more quickly than Briggs had anticipated, and, perhaps emboldened by the day's consumption of beer, rushed Freddie's right flank like an angry bull rhino. Ferguson connected solidly, and this time, both men sailed to the ground in a heap. Freddie landed first, his left arm extended as Ferguson's mass drove him to the floor. The men rolled around, their arms and legs entwined like giant sequoias tangled together. They crashed into small two-top tables, sending pitchers of beer and glasses to the floor, where they shattered in a tinkling symphony.

The heat in Freddie's belly exploded, like leaking natural gas catching a spark. He could feel the big man tiring; as big as Ferguson was, he was woefully out of shape. His rabbit punches grew exponentially weaker, and Freddie could feel him gasping huge lungfuls of air. Freddie wrapped his good arm around Ferguson's midsection and flipped him over like a side of beef; then he leapt astride Ferguson's midsection and delivered a right cross to the man's face, his big fist slamming down like a pile driver. The punch crashed into Ferguson's nose, squashing it like an overripe tomato. Ferguson grunted as a tincture of blood bloomed outwards from his face, holding its shape, a crimson rose, for an instant, before raining down on his shirt in a messy splatter.

Freddie reared back to deliver another blow when he heard a commotion behind him. A quick turn of his head, some movement in the corner of his eye, and that was when he felt a sharp burning sensation at the back of his neck. His entire body seized up, like his brain had issued his muscles a lockdown order, and that was when the world went dark.

Hashtag #Flu

August 6

1:16 p.m. to 1:18 p.m. Eastern Daylight Time

@RoseLover: Worried about my neighbor. He was c/o #flu symptoms yesterday. Ambulance came today. Hope he's better soon! #bronx #influenza

@AbbyWeinstein: I live in the #Bronx. A LOT of my neighbors are really sick. Maybe #flu?

@NYHotMama: Boss is sick with #flu, got to leave work early! #Booya! #philly

@BigRigger: This #flu's hitting me hard. Scheduled to head out on long haul 2morrow. Wish I could rest up, but gotta work.

@GoYanks55: Feel like sheeeeeit. Thought it was too early for #flu season! LOL!

@LovePS3: Summer school cancelled this afternoon 'cuz Teach is sick with #flu! Hellz to the yeah!

@TomZapata: #Doctors out there? Saw a weird strain of #flu-like illness in Queens last night. hit me w/ @ reply if you've seen it.

@BlogginBobby: RIP, Carl Hubbard. My uncle died today of the #flu. Came out of nowhere.

∾

From CNN's Facebook Page

August 6

3:31 p.m. to 3:33 p.m. Eastern Daylight Time

CNN is tracking a possible outbreak of influenza in the Northeast. Do you or does someone you know have the flu? Leave a comment!

Thuy Beltran

My husband got very sick very fast. We are in hospital. He had fever 106 degrees!

Megan Waddell

I'm an ER nurse in the Bronx. We were slammed overnight with patients. High fevers, pneumonia-type illness. Multiple deaths. Scared.

Eric Martin

I've got a terrible sore throat. I don't feel too hot right now. I've been traveling a lot for work. I always get sick after a long business trip!

Michael Horton

I bet the government's behind it! We're all doomed! lol

Carolyn Mixon

My brother is a doctor in Philadelphia. He's worried about this outbreak. He won't say much. Any doctors out there?

From the New York Times, Online Edition

By CLYDE MORGAN

New York Times Staff Writer

Posted to nytimes.com @ 11:59 p.m. Eastern Daylight Time on Saturday, August 7

DEADLY FLU HITTING THE BRONX

THE BRONX – At least three Bronx-area hospitals are dealing with a deadly flu-like illness that has claimed dozens of lives in the past day, raising concern among New York City medical professionals that a novel and lethal strain of influenza has emerged. Calls to the Bronx Health District and the New York State Health Department earlier this evening were not immediately returned.

A physician at one of the hospitals, speaking on the condition of anonymity, reported he had never seen anything like it in two decades as a physician.

"We're overwhelmed," the doctor reported. "We just got slammed one morning with patients and it hasn't let up. Young, old, all races, all ethnicities. I've never seen anything like it before in my life. I suspect it's viral, but that's a total guess on my part. We notified the state health department and we're just trying to ride it out, hope it doesn't get worse."

The doctor further reported that the hospital has established a quarantine unit in the facility, as there are some fears in the hospital that the illness is airborne. The doctor confirmed that symptoms of the virus include sore throat, high fever, seizures, and internal bleeding.

"This thing is a monster," he reported. He urged anyone in the New York City area experiencing these symptoms to be examined by a physician.

All three hospitals refused to comment, citing patient privacy concerns.

4

The knocking at the door was firm and insistent, the kind of sharp rapping that said this late-night visitor didn't really want to be knocking on your door at one-thirty in the morning, but they really had a good reason, and if you could help them out *just this one time*, they'd be forever grateful. Adam was awake and nursing a scotch, dressed in a pair of Syracuse University lacrosse shorts. He was watching *Goodfellas* on DVD, about a third of the way through, the scene in which Ray Liotta's character pistol-whips Lorraine Bracco's old boyfriend from her snooty country club.

He set down the scotch and remembered he was shirtless. As he looked for his misplaced shirt, the knocking ceased, and he wondered whether his visitor had simply given up, or perhaps, had decided he was banging on the wrong door.

A few seconds later, the knocking resumed, more frantic this time, as if whomever was out there had seen a gaggle of zombies closing in. Screw it, Adam thought, abandoning his search for the shirt. His guest was just going to have to deal with his pale, mealy upper body. Adam stepped out into the corridor and made his way to the front door. He pressed an eye to the peephole and, in the spill of the yellow porch light, saw a middle-aged woman, her eyes wide with panic, repeatedly running her fingers through her long brown hair. Her lips were pressed tightly together. Adam instantly recognized the look on her face; as a physician, he saw it almost every day in the faces of patients waiting for test results. He opened the door a crack, fairly certain this woman meant him no harm (because no one who wanted to slit your throat in the middle of the night knocked first, right?), but just a crack because you just never knew these days.

Adam opened the door, but she didn't notice. Her head was turned north, and she was tapping a finger against her lips. She wore a pair of green shorts and a grey sweatshirt on this cool night.

When he cleared his throat to let her know he was standing there, she jumped and let out a little scream. When her eyes met Adam's, she planted a hand over her chest and let out a long sigh, as if she'd been holding her breath for a while.

"Oh, thank God you're home," she said. "You're a doctor, right?"

"Yes," Adam said. "How did you-"

"The sticker on your car," she said. "We noticed it the other day."

"Right," Adam said, remembering the hospital-issued Physician parking sticker on the rear bumper of his truck.

"My family and I are staying two doors down," she said. "I'm sorry to bother you so late, but my husband is really, really sick. I called an ambulance, but they said it might be twenty minutes before they can get here. Twenty minutes!"

"I'd be glad to, but I've had a few drinks," Adam said. "You're probably better off waiting for the ambulance."

"Please, I don't care," she said, her hands clenched at her chest, almost in prayer.

"What's the problem?"

"He's burning up, and he's bleeding from the eyes, ears and mouth."

"Sure, sure," Adam said, trying to mask his alarm at the symptoms the woman had just described. "Let me get some clothes on?"

"Oh," the woman said, the question catching her off guard. "Oh. Yes, of course."

Adam slipped back inside the house to get dressed, his juices flowing, his mind on high alert, in a good way. He'd been at the cottage for three days, living a primal existence: eating, drinking, sleeping and shitting. His supplies would last him for at least another week, and so he hadn't had to leave the cottage. He hadn't bothered checking news or e-mail, because quite frankly, he'd started to enjoy not hearing the same stories reheated like leftovers and spun out to the hungry audiences desperate for another salacious detail about this child murder or that political scandal. He'd been drinking a lot, probably more than he should have, but what the hell – everyone was entitled to a bender every now and again, right?

As he pulled on a shirt and sandals, he considered the man's symptoms. Bleeding from one of those orifices wasn't alarming in and of itself, but bleeding from all three was not a good sign. Before exiting his bedroom, he snagged a pair of latex gloves from a box he kept in the closet.

Adam closed the door behind him and followed the woman downstairs. As they made their way up the road, Adam trailed behind a length. It didn't seem appropriate to walk side-by-side on this beach road. That was for husbands and wives, boyfriends and girl-friends, families headed for a day by the ocean.

They walked in silence for another twenty yards, and she turned up a wide driveway leading to a large home, her pace quickening as she slalomed around a Toyota Sequoia parked in the carport. The home was set closer to the water than Adam's cottage, and it provided a spectacular vista of the ocean. The moon was full tonight, a large coin hanging in the inky blackness of space, its shine cutting a long shimmery path across the top of the water. The night was awash in the crash of waves against the beach, just a little bit to their south. By the time they'd made it up to the expansive front deck of the house, she was weeping, her shoulders heaving up and down.

"What's your name?" Adam asked as she swung the screen door open.

"Katie," she said. "Katie Sanders. We're from Annapolis."

"I'm Adam Fisher," he said.

"It's nice to meet you, Dr. Fisher," she said.

"Hey, we're on vacation," he said. "You can call me Adam here."

This earned a smile, Adam was relieved to see. He had no idea what was in store for him on the other side of this door, but things would go a lot more smoothly if Katie Sanders remained calm.

"Sorry for busting in on you like this," Katie said. "I just didn't know what to do. He started getting sick at lunchtime. It seemed like he was just coming down with a cold, and then things just went down from there. I've never seen him so sick. I've never seen anyone so sick."

Adam nodded.

"Let's go on in and have a look."

ADAM KNEW THINGS WERE BAD, possibly even worse than Katie Sanders from Annapolis had feared, as soon as they stepped inside. They were in the kitchen, quiet but clean, bright and awash in fluorescent light. A peninsula-style countertop separated the kitchen from an eat-in area and served as the home base for the array of snacks fueling any good beach vacation. A large bag of potato chips sealed shut with a plastic chip clip that looked like a pair of bright red lips. Two trays of store-bought cookies were stacked at the edge of the counter. A six-pack of bottled water and two bottles of wine.

Despite the home's outwardly cheery appearance, the air was stuffy and rank, the sweet stench of something that has just turned over hanging thickly in the air. He hated the smell, not because it nauseated him (because it didn't), but because it meant he had already lost. He knew the smell from his hospital's intensive care unit, where his patients occasionally ended up and often never left. It was subtle, like a woman's perfume dabbed on the inside of her wrists, easily missed.

It was the smell of death.

"He's over here," Katie said, pointing toward a room around the corner from the kitchen.

Adam crossed through the living room, where two teenagers sat on the floral-print couch. The older one, a girl, had her knees drawn up to her chest and was chewing her nails. Her brother, maybe thirteen, was sitting next to the girl and was staring at his hands. The television was on, tuned to CNN, but the volume was muted.

"These are our kids," Katie said. "Leigh and Chris."

Adam nodded toward them. He didn't see the need to dispense empty pleasantries. They nodded back, in simpatico with Adam's desire to remain silent.

A pathetic moan from the bedroom broke the silence. The girl drew her knees in even more tightly, as if she was trying to make herself disappear, and tears began streaming down her face. The boy sat stone still, his eyes down, his hands folded on his lap.

"Is he going to be okay?" the boy asked, never looking up from his hands.

"I'm here to help," Adam said. He had not answered the boy's question, defaulting instead to a weak platitude that didn't mean a whole hell of a lot. He didn't know what else to say. Maybe something stronger, a potent elixir of encouragement that would have eased these kids' worrying, but he couldn't bring himself to do it.

"Doctor?" she said softly, dipping her head toward the closed bedroom door.

She rapped twice on the door, and called out: "Terry? Honey, I've got a doctor here to see you."

She swung the door in toward the bedroom. From his vantage point at the threshold, Adam could see a figure prone on the bed, buried under about ten blankets. The odor was stronger here, a sourness in the air. Adam pulled on the latex gloves and approached his patient.

"Terry?" Adam said, sitting on the bed next to the man. "I'm Dr. Fisher. Your wife says you're slacking off on the chores, wants me to make sure you're actually sick."

The man did not respond, but it did draw a half-chuckle, half-sob from Katie Sanders. It never ceased to amaze Adam. No matter how dire, how bleak things were, a well-placed joke mocking the crappy situation in which his patients and their loved ones found themselves often bonded them to Adam. It seemed a little phony to Adam, but he could not deny it reinforced the doctor-patient relationship like concrete rebar.

Adam peeled back the blankets far enough to expose the man's face, and a chill ran up his spine when he saw it. Terry Sanders was bright, almost shiny, with fever; Adam could feel the heat radiating from his body, as if he were standing too close to a hot oven. Blood had caked around his nostrils and his ears, and it was trickling from the corners of his mouth. It gave him a horrifying visage. Older blood had dried and caked to a rusty brown on the pillowcases. Adam ran his fingers along the underside of the man's jaw and found the glands to be badly swollen, like the spine of a wet paperback book. His cheeks were sunken, and his eyes were cloudy. The man had clearly developed some sort of infection, but that diagnosis was about as specific as saying that the man was sick. Without tests, there was no way to know whether the infection was viral, bacterial or fungal. Hell, it could have been a case of severe food poisoning.

"Mr. Sanders?" Adam called out, loudly and firmly. "Can you hear me?"

Terry Sanders was curled up in the fetal position, his face turned upward toward the ceiling. It looked tremendously uncomfortable, but he didn't seem to care, which only underscored the level of misery the man was experiencing. Adam touched the man's forehead with the back of his hand and jerked it away. The man was roasting with fever; Adam would have gambled his medical license on a reading of at least 105 degrees, a terrifying reading for an adult.

"When did you say he started getting sick?" Adam asked as he continued to examine Terry Sanders. He didn't look up at Katie because he didn't want her to see the look of hopelessness he was certain was plastered across his face. To keep himself busy, he checked the man's pulse, which was weak and erratic, like a radio signal from deep space.

"Let me think," she said. "Lunchtime. He mentioned he had a sore throat, chills, that kind of thing. He napped most of the afternoon and evening, and then he started coughing up blood about an hour ago."

Adam did the math. Twelve hours from the onset of flulike symptoms to death's door. He racked his brain, trying to remember what he knew about infectious diseases from medical school and the random conference where he was trying to catch up on his continuing education requirements. This wasn't his specialty.

"Anyone else sick?" he asked.

"I don't think so," she said, her voice growing louder with each successive word. "Is it contagious? What's going on?"

"I'm just asking right now," Adam said. "First things first. We need to try and get his fever down a little. It's not good for it to be this high."

"Why is he so sick? What's wrong with him?"

Adam took a deep breath and let it out slowly.

"I don't know," Adam said. "I need you to get me a wet washcloth. Cool water. Not too cold. We need to bring it down slowly. And some ibuprofen or Tylenol."

"I gave him some Advil an hour ago."

"Jesus," Adam whispered to himself. "Any antibiotics in the house?"

She shook her head.

"The washcloth, then," he said.

Katie Sanders nodded, pressing a tight fist against her lips and closing her eyes. Adam could tell she was trying to keep her wits about her even as her psyche was fracturing like glass. She left the room, leaving Adam alone with Terry Sanders. He could hear a brief discussion in the living room as the children sought a status update on their father.

Adam took in the room while he waited for his putative nurse to return. It was a standard beach cottage bedroom, sparsely furnished with a rarely used chest of drawers and a flat-screen television mounted in the corner. A penciled rendition of a Holden Beach map hung over the bed.

He checked on the patient again, pressing the back of his hand against Terry's cheek. Still scorching hot, like the man was chewing on a lit match. Adam couldn't recall ever encountering a patient with a fever this high. As he pulled his hand back, Terry started seizing, as if his whole body was experiencing a massive internal earthquake. Adam gently rolled him over onto his side and held him there as his body quivered and heaved, flopping around like a fish in the bottom of a boat. It stretched on interminably. In all his years as a physician, Adam had never seen a seizure go on for so long, had never seen one so violent. Finally, mercifully, it ended, leaving Terry Sanders on his back, his eyes open and glassy and staring at the ceiling.

"Terry?" Adam said. Then again, very loudly this time, Adam no longer concerned with whether he might frighten Mrs. Sanders or her children: "Terry?"

No response. Not a twitch.

Terry Sanders was dead.

INTERLUDE

FROM ATC RECORDINGS OF SKYDANCE AIRLINES FLIGHT 337

August 7

8:53 p.m. Pacific Daylight Time

310 Miles South-Southwest of Los Angeles International Airport

L.A. Center – Skydance three-three-seven heavy, we're gonna have EMS out to meet you.

Skydance 337 – Three-three-seven, L.A. Center, it's getting worse.

L.A. Center – Repeat that, three-three-seven heavy.

Skydance 337 – Franks is dead.

L.A. Center – What about Meadows?

Skydance 337 – I feel like shit, Tower.

L.A. Center – Hey, three-three-seven heavy, check your airspeed. What about Meadows?

Skydance 337 – Roger. Meadows is asleep. Can't seem to wake him up.

L.A. Center – Three-three-seven heavy, your airspeed is a little low. How are the passengers?

Skydance 337 – [WHEEZING COUGH] Jesus. Hurts. It's quiet back there. Not sure if that's a bad or good thing.

L.A. Center – You listen, we're gonna take care of you, three-three-seven. You'll be on the ground in forty minutes. But you've got to give me a little gas here. Put the nose down a bit, just a hair.

Skydance 337 – Gonna climb a bit.

L.A. Center – Negative, three-three-seven heavy, negative. Oh, fuck!

Skydance 337 – [WHOOP! WHOOP! STALL WARNING. WHOOP! WHOOP! STALL WARNING.]

L.A. Center – Nose down, three-three-seven.

Skydance 337 – We're stalled, we're stalled! [LONG SPELL OF COUGHING]

L.A. Center – Ease up on the stick, three-three-seven. You're making it worse!

Skydance 337 – [Unintelligible]

L.A. Center – Nose down, Jesus Christ, three-three-seven, nose down.

Skydance 337 – I don't feel good. [Unintelligible]

At 8:55 p.m. PDT on August 7, Skydance Airlines Flight 337, carrying 238 passengers and crew, disappeared from radar.

5

Dr. William Ponce thought he'd known what it meant to be truly scared.

He thought he'd been scared when his son Alex, then three, had choked on a chunk of apple, the little boy pawing at his throat, his face turning red and then blue, as if Ponce was being treated to the worst fireworks display of all time, the pyrotechnics show someone might see on his first night in hell. But as awful as it was, the episode had lasted less than twenty seconds, ending when his wife Molly had delivered just the right force of slap to dislodge the malicious chunk of fruit and send it flying across the room. Alex was a typical sixteen-year-old now, having no memory of how close he'd come to dying before his fourth birthday.

And as the chief pathologist for the U.S. Army's

Medical Research Institute for Infectious Disease, he was quite familiar with fear – it was part of the job description. He was fifty-five now, having spent nearly two decades at Fort Detrick in Maryland, working alongside some of the most lethal agents known to man. He still remembered popping his Ebola cherry, his first trip inside Biosafety Level 4 now twenty-five years gone by, when he'd participated in the necropsy of a monkey that had died of Ebola Zaire, the most terrifying organism he'd ever encountered (until two days ago, at least). As they'd examined the liquefied tissue inside that poor monkey (and he still thought about that monkey a quarter century later), his heart had pounded at his chest wall like a meth-fueled jack-hammer, threatening to fracture him from the inside out, the virus-laden blood seeping out of the ruined corpse as they worked on it. But that had been restrictor plate racing, the fear capped by the spacesuit he wore, the precautions they took, the strict protocols in place to prevent any breach of the integrity of the equipment or the facility.

He remembered all the stupid things he'd once worried about, like tearing his suit inside Level 4, disappointing his new bosses at USAMRIID, even panicking inside the spacesuit, which occasionally happened to newbies in 4. Every now and again, a rookie would rip off the space helmet inside the hottest of the lab's hot zones because they'd convinced themselves they were suffocating even though subsequent testing showed the oxygen had been moving freely inside the suit.

In his two-plus decades assigned to USAMRIID, he'd never developed spacesuit fever, as they called it, but he did dream about the viruses, big, bright dreams of accidental sticks from needles dripping with Ebola-tainted monkey blood, or taking a face-full of the black vomit that accompanied the end stage of Marburg infection. Then he'd wake up, bathed in sweat but a dozen miles from Level 4, his bedroom quiet but for the gurgle of the fish tank. He didn't even mind the dreams so much; it was, he supposed, his mind's way of letting off steam, relieving the pressure of working in Level 4.

Only now though, as he sipped his coffee alone in USAMRIID's main conference room, a Baltimore Orioles mug clutched in a trembling hand, did he know what it meant to be truly afraid. The difference, he realized on that humid August morning, was that this wasn't a trip inside Level 4 from the safety of the Racal spacesuit, where the fear was of the hypothetical, always a *What If* question. This was something else entirely, a presence, consuming him from the inside out, eating away at his sanity, threatening to destroy his ability to think coherently before he could even attempt to do anything about this mess. It had transcended the hypothetical into the very fucking real. A real American city, population 1.5 million – the Bronx, for Chrissakes! – had become, for all intents and purposes, an open-air Level 4. It was out there *right now*, spreading from person to person, and there was nothing he could do about it.

The twenty-six-inch monitor in front of him, emblazoned with the seal of the President of the United States, flickered briefly and then showed a long view of the White House Situation Room. President Crosby's chair at the head of the table was empty, but every other chair was occupied, their occupants chit-chatting about *This Important Problem* or *That Important Problem*. He recognized some of the faces from their appearances on the various cable and online news outlets, but the only person he knew by name was Kevin Butler, the White House Chief of Staff, seated just to the left of the President's chair. Butler was leafing through a dossier that had been delivered to the White House in a screaming caravan of black Suburbans, hand-carried by the USAMRIID director himself.

Ponce could just make out his reflection on the screen, and it was not a flattering one. He hadn't shaved in two days, and he haired up like a Yeti. The circles under his eyes were dark and getting darker. Exhaustion held him tightly in its grip, but the fear kept him awake, a never-ending electric charge. As he took a deep breath to calm himself, he heard the sound of a door opening; all twelve men and women around the conference table leapt to their feet as President Nathan Crosby swooped into the room.

Crosby cut an impressive figure, well over six feet tall, still handsome despite three rough years in office, his only concession to the advancing years a bit of gray edging up his temples. Ponce didn't like him, thought he was a dipshit, someone who'd cruised into office on a relentless wave of campaign ads blasting his predecessor for what he had been unable to do, not anything Crosby had actually planned to do. Ponce didn't hold politicians in very high esteem to begin with, but this guy, the former governor of Oklahoma, really took the cake with his anti-vaccination stance, his tirades against evolution, his general tolerance for stupidity because Ponce believed stupid people had put Nathan Crosby into office. Not that his predecessor had been any better. When you got right down to it, the country was a bit of a mess, wobbling from one recession to another like a lost child (even though no one wanted to use the word 'depression'). Crosby was up for re-election in November; he was in a statistical dead heat with his scrappy Democratic opponent.

The President leaned over to Butler and whispered something; both men laughed. This made Ponce's blood boil and all but confirmed what he was worried about. They were not taking this outbreak seriously.

"Dr. Ponce?" Butler said. "President Crosby will hear your report now."

"Good morning, Mr. President," Ponce said, clearing his throat. He pressed a button on a small remote, transmitting the three-dimensional scan of the virus to a 50-inch LED screen in the Situation Room, adjacent to the videoconference screen. The virus, which they had code-named Medusa, looked like a long curlicue, not terribly dissimilar to a snake, coiled and ready to strike.

"I wish I had better news, sir," Ponce said. "This is the Medusa virus you see on the monitor, magnified about fifty thousand times. The mortality rate is in excess of ninety-five percent, perhaps even higher. We've got fifty-six confirmed cases. Fifty-one are dead, and the other five are circling the drain."

"How far has the outbreak spread?" Butler asked.

"We're not entirely sure about that," Ponce said. "The CDC is tracking unconfirmed reports of the illness in eleven states, but the epicenter of the outbreak appears to be in the Bronx. Until we can confirm that, probably in the next day or so, the CDC and USAMRIID both recommend quarantining the affected areas. There's still time to limit the loss of life. Anyone infected with the virus probably doesn't feel well enough to travel far."

"Quarantines?" Butler bellowed. "Dr. Ponce, do you

have any idea how much of a cluster fuck quarantines will be?"

"But sir-"

"Nearly two million people live in the Bronx alone," Butler said, his voice tinged with annoyance. "People will fucking panic. We can't go around screaming that the sky is falling like happened with the swine flu thing. We have to step carefully here. The President is in a sensitive position."

Oh, shit, Ponce thought, the picture crystallizing in front of him like the virus coming into clear focus under the scope. This wasn't just a matter of them not taking him seriously. They were viewing this outbreak through the prism of politics, the number of votes that this would cost him if he made a misstep. Ponce recalled the H1N1 outbreak back in 2009, which, in the end, had claimed only about 30,000 lives – a blip on the radar as far as pandemics went. But that hadn't been during an election year. Crosby's Democratic challenger had been hammering him as soft, indecisive, a political development along the lines of the Three Little Pigs threatening to blow down the Big Bad Wolf's house. Now, Ponce knew, Crosby was worried that if he overreacted to this outbreak, he'd be a dead man walking come the first Tuesday in November.

"Mr. President," Ponce said, going over Butler's head and directing his plea directly to the big guy, "I can assure you that this is not going to be like the swine flu thing."

It was a calculated risk, a big one; he'd emasculated Kevin Butler (and it had felt pretty good), but he'd pushed all his chips to the center of the table on this hand. If this didn't work, there was nowhere else to go. Ponce kept his gaze squarely on Crosby, but he could sense Butler cooking with anger.

"How is the virus transmitted?" asked Crosby.

"We're working on that, sir," Ponce said. "Direct exposure to blood and bodily fluids, we know that. I'm virtually certain it's airborne, but I don't have confirmation of that yet."

The words were out of Ponce's mouth before he could stop himself. He had intended to fudge the fact, he had intended to lie his ass off about it because it was the right thing to do. Lie about it, lie about it to the President of the United States so they would take him seriously until he could positively confirm something he knew to be true anyway.

"You haven't confirmed this is an airborne strain?" Butler asked, jumping back into the discussion.

Ponce wanted to punch himself in the face for his stupidity; he felt like he was outside his own body, staring down at the big, stupid idiot, the idiot with the M.D. and double doctorates in virology and pathology.

"No, sir, but we will this afternoon at the latest, and

I think we need to err on the side of caution given how deadly the infection has proven to be."

Ponce's words hung in the air as his audience considered them.

"These viruses," Crosby said, "they're not typically airborne are they?"

"No, sir," Ponce said, his shoulders sagging.

"These outbreaks burn themselves out, isn't that right?" Crosby asked. "That's why Ebola has never blown up and wiped us out, why it stays in those African villages."

"No one is really sure why-" Ponce offered.

"But they do, right?"

"Yes, sir, but I'm incredibly concerned this may not burn-"

"As am I, Dr. Ponce," Crosby said. "As am I. That's why I want to leave the management of these outbreaks to the local health departments. It's our belief they're in the best position to implement the appropriate protocols to contain the outbreak."

"But sir," Ponce said, again trying to establish a beachhead against the formidable defenses in the room.

"Dr. Ponce," Butler said, finding a second wind, "you're familiar with the phrase, 'the cure is worse than the disease'?"

"Of course."

"We believe a quarantine is premature at this time

and in fact could do more harm than good," Butler said. "People will panic. We'll have looting, riots. It'll devastate the economy, and that's not something we can afford right now."

Dr. Ponce couldn't believe his ears. He ran his hands back and forth through his hair, thick and gray and wild, racking his brain for some way to get through to these morons. He was blowing it. This was the most important presentation of his life, and he was absolutely blowing it! With panic replicating in his core like the very virus he was trying to combat, he flipped through the file on the table in front of him, looking for something, anything that might shake these guys up. There, he thought, putting his hands on a photograph in the file.

"Look here," he said, holding the eight-by-ten photograph up to the camera. "Look at this. This is Dr. Amanda Rutledge. She was on staff at the New York City Health Department in the Bronx. Her husband, Peter Rutledge, worked for the Yankees. Three days ago, Mr. Rutledge began showing symptoms of Medusa and died twelve hours later."

The President held up a finger as if he were going to say something, but he remained silent.

"When they opened him up," Ponce continued, "they discovered evidence of tremendous hemorrhaging and organ liquefaction," Butler said. "His lungs were a mess, just totally fucking vaporized."

Yes, he had just dropped the F-bomb to the President of the United States.

"Mr. President, this is the part you need to know, that I need you to understand," Ponce said, as if he were lecturing a kindergartner. He had probably crossed the line over to insubordination, but he didn't care. He could have told President Crosby that Dr. Rutledge's boss, the director of the Bronx district, had died this morning, or he could have told him the two CDC doctors who had traveled to New York were both infected with Medusa and would be dead by lunchtime. He could have told him they'd be burying millions of Americans in the next month, but that seemed too surreal, too much to grasp. Instead, he zoomed in up-close. All politics are local.

"Dr. Rutledge died yesterday, as did her three children, ages nine, eleven and fifteen," Ponce said, his eyes squarely on the President, ignoring everyone else in the room. It no longer mattered what they thought; all he had to do was convince Crosby, the big kahuna. Crosby had two boys of his own, roughly the same age as the elder Rutledge children. If Ponce couldn't penetrate the formidable political armor, perhaps he could get through to the man as a father; it was the last arrow in his quiver.

"They all died horrible, horrific deaths," Ponce said, panicked. "Scared shitless. Begging for their mom, who they didn't even know was dead. Screaming, burning with fever, coughing up blood and lung tissue, bleeding from the eyes and ears until they had seizures, big massive seizures that all but fried their central nervous systems."

For a moment, like a flash of heat lightning in the distance, Ponce thought he saw the tiniest crack in the President's political visage, the ordered and carefully prescribed face of calm and leadership that he showed the world. For a moment, Butler thought he'd won the man over, that they might have a chance to stop this thing before it got out of control.

Ponce sat stone still, watching the President carefully. Crosby's hands were clenched together in a fist, tapping his lips nervously. Butler leaned in close, whispered something to the President, who nodded.

"Dr. Ponce," Butler said. "At this time, the President is going to leave incident management in the hands of the locals. The President, however, wants hourly reports on the situation, more if the situation warrants."

Dammit, Ponce thought. They'd known all along what they were going to do, and now they could use the CDC's inability to confirm the airborne spread of the virus to massage the crisis so it fit their desired outcome. They couldn't even use the word "outbreak." *Situation*, Butler had called it. *Incident*. Fucking cowards.

"If there's nothing else," Butler said. "Thank you, Dr. Ponce."

Ponce was tongue-tied, a million things he wanted to say screaming through his brain but freezing on the launch pad, getting tangled together like strands of Christmas lights. He mumbled something in reply to Butler, and that was that. The link to the Situation Room was severed, and Ponce found himself looking at the Presidential seal again for a moment, until that, too, vanished.

He stared at the blank television screen for a very long time.

6

Adam sat on his deck, drinking coffee and smoking cigarettes from a crumpled pack he'd found in his car. He didn't smoke often, but the thing with Sanders family had rattled him badly and had been playing on a constant loop in his head for the last three days. A gnawing sensation tickled his gut like a termite chewing away a wooden floor joist, telling him he'd screwed something up again, that he should've handled the situation differently.

As Adam delivered the bad news to Katie Sanders, he could hear water from the cool-not-cold washcloth in her hand dripping onto the carpet in wet squishy plops. She'd become hysterical, collapsing to the floor, wailing and crying. When the ambulance arrived some five minutes later, Adam spoke with the paramedics, told him he was a physician, tried to explain what had happened, even though he wasn't entirely sure what that was. Katie and her two children followed the ambulance in their car as it made its way east on Ocean Boulevard toward the causeway, leaving everything behind as if they'd just gone up the road a piece to hit Island Mini-Golf for nine holes under the oversized gorilla and grab a soft-serve cone. He'd stood on their deck, alone, for nearly an hour before he ambled back to the house, a healthy dose of shock wrapped around him like a beach towel.

Adam fixed himself his third cup of coffee, or maybe it was his fourth, and settled back into the Adirondack chair to watch the sun start its daily journey into the sky. Daybreak started as a glimmer of light, as if the morning gloom had sprung a leak around its bottom edge, before exploding into every corner and crevice, every nook and cranny, jolting the East Coast back to life. The ocean air was already swampy and thick with brine; it was going to be a hell of a hot day.

He found it indescribably and ludicrously sad that this terrible thing had happened to the Sanders during their vacation. As if it would have been any easier on them had Terry been good enough to wait until they'd gotten home to drown on his own blood, after the suntans had faded, after the inevitable seafood feast, its newspapers spread out for the mess left behind by the crab legs and lobster claws and shrimp cocktail.

He thought about all the shit Katie Sanders would be facing upon their return to Paramus or Reading or Timonium or wherever it was she said that they were from, piled on top of her excruciating grief. The phone calls to stunned relatives and friends, the planning of a funeral, preparing for a life without Terry, when her biggest concern had once been that Terry's little bug might put a little crimp in the family's vacation schedule. Unexpected death was brutal in its assault on the lives of the survivors, the permanent rupture of happiness twinned with the cold machinery of death. It was the ultimate inconvenience.

Adam's eyelids drooped. The caffeine and nicotine kept his synapses firing, artificial adrenaline, but he didn't think it was doing much for him, no more good than paddles applied to a non-responsive heart. He felt the exhaustion deep within his core. The stress of the last few days, starting with the letter from the Board of Medicine and capped off with Sanders' death, was getting to him. He staggered to the bedroom and fell asleep almost immediately.

He woke up around two in the afternoon, amazed he'd slept as long as he did. He was on his stomach, his arm pinned underneath his head, and as he rolled over onto his back, he felt the pins and needles as the nerve endings started firing again. After a quick lunch of a peanut butter and banana sandwich, he decided to get down to the beach for a couple of hours. He could feel it calling to him, the sound of the waves crashing on the shore, delivering the coastline an eternal beating, a salve for what ailed him.

As he changed into his trunks, he couldn't help but wonder about his own exposure to whatever pathogen had killed the family's patriarch. But he reminded himself that even if Terry had a communicable disease, he'd probably experienced a rare complication, unique to his particular physiology. It was entirely possible that Terry Sanders died of garden-variety influenza. That he'd just pulled a rotten card, winning the kind of lottery no one wants to win.

He briefly considered driving back to Richmond, but decided against it. Back in Virginia, he'd be stuck in his stuffy house, unable to work, stuck in a no–man's land between clock-punchers and vacationers, alone with nothing but the memories of what had happened here. As the sun brightened the house with a fresh dose of light, he decided to stick it out.

He went back out on the porch and noticed it was a lot cooler than it had been this morning. The deck was dark with wetness, rain that had fallen while he slept. A bright blue sky extended as far as he could see in each direction, the view unclouded with haze, like a clean windshield. He looked out over his railing toward the sea, calm but for the small waves lapping to the shore, the air fresh and clean. Perfect conditions for a run on the beach. As he scanned the oceanfront, trying to decide which direction he'd head, something about the scene started nagging him, like a phantom eyelash digging in his eye.

After a quick change into his running clothes, opting to go barefoot, he made his way out the front door and curled around the side to the beach access. Although Adam had an unobstructed view of the ocean, he didn't have direct access to the beach because of the ridge of protected dunes that his house backed up to. He set out up the wooden sidewalk, down onto the sand, and then turned east along the water's edge.

A minute into his run, just as his muscles had started to loosen up, Adam stopped in ankle-deep surf, the mental eyelash dislodging itself. The beach was virtually deserted. His heart started throbbing, a visceral reaction to a scene that was wrong, all wrong. It was two-thirty on a beautiful August afternoon, and there should have been dozens, no, hundreds of people out here, sunning themselves, splashing in the water, building sand castles, sneaking illegal beers in those little huggies.

There was nobody out here.

The empty beach left Adam disoriented. It was as if his mind was straining to see what should have been there, what he, in his medical practice, would call *within normal limits*. As the unease grew inside him, his eyes bounced from water to sand to the cottages lining the oceanfront and then back to the water. A bit farther down the beach, he saw a group of empty beach chairs, set up in a semi-circle, but no one around them.

The image of Terry Sanders dying in his beach cottage slammed into Adam's head like a drunk running a red light. He looked at the houses up and down the oceanfront, from the small cottages to the big ten-bedroom jobs with wraparound decks on each floor and pictured Terry Sanders in each of those houses, coughing up blood, seizing, his organs frying inside his overheated body.

He picked up a flicker in the corner of his eye, and he turned to face it. Maybe a hundred yards away, two people were walking toward him. From this distance, he couldn't make out their gender, age, or really anything about them at all. Still, it was something. With his heart pounding, he walked, accelerating to a jog before breaking into a full sprint in their direction.

As he approached them, the pair started coming into focus. A heavyset guy, maybe in his mid-forties, a tall, skinny teenager trailing behind him. The older guy wasn't walking as much as he was staggering across the sand like a drunken pirate who'd forgotten where he'd buried his treasure. The boy, trailing behind, didn't seem terribly concerned with the older man's behavior.

"Excuse me?" Adam called out. "Are you guys OK?"

The man stopped and looked at Adam, his mouth opening and closing but not making any sound. He was wearing dark red swim trunks and nothing else, his large gut stretching the waistband of his suit. His arms and legs were deeply tanned, but his chest and neck were fiery red with sunburn. It was quite the contrast, the reddish pink of burnt flesh juxtaposed against the leathery skin of his extremities, brown from years in the sun. That was when Adam noticed the man's mouth was stained red, almost like he'd been eating a cherry snow cone.

"No," Adam heard himself saying, feeling his body go weak. "No. This can't be happening."

His legs buckled, and he dropped to his knees.

Adam and the man stared at each other a bit longer, up until a coughing spasm grabbed the man in its clutches. He doubled over at the knees as his body fought to clear out whatever obstruction was stopping up his lungs. The first spasm ended, giving the guy a chance to catch his breath before a second one exploded, this one far worse than the first. Blood sprayed from his mouth like he'd been shot in the throat, and he dropped to his knees as well. Adam's training took over, and he pushed himself to his feet.

"You," Adam said, pointing at the boy, whose face was blank. "Is this your father?"

The boy nodded vigorously.

"What's your name?"

"Ethan," the boy said. "Ethan DeSilva." He was tall and thin and sported a thick mane of greasy black hair. He was fair-skinned, but his current complexion looked much worse, an almost grayed-out pallor.

"And your dad?"

"Robert DeSilva."

"What's going on?" Adam asked. "How long's he been sick?"

"Since last night I think," Ethan said, stifling his own cough.

Adam helped Robert down to his seat. He looked up at Adam, his eyes virtually pleading for help. Adam ran his fingers along Robert's jawbone and found over-sized glands, engaged in a desperate war to fight off a pathogen. Typically, Adam would listen to a patient's chest, but that wasn't necessary here. He could hear the rattling in Robert's chest even over the small waves lapping at the shore.

"Just you two down here at Holden?"

"No," Ethan said. "My mom and two sisters. We're all feeling pretty bad. I've got a fever and chills. An hour ago, he just up and bolted out the front door."

"How far up the beach are you?"

Ethan looked over his shoulder and stared into the distance. When he looked back, his eyes were glossy with tears.

"I don't remember," Ethan said. "I really don't feel very good."

Adam scraped a nail against his chin rhythmically, almost like a metronome.

"My cottage isn't far from here," he said after a minute. "Let's get you guys to the hospital. I'm going to need your help to get your dad there."

It took them twenty minutes to cover the two hundred yards back to Adam's cottage. Robert was unable to stand up on his own, his body ravaged by a series of innard-shredding coughing spells. Ethan was weakening by the minute. He began yelling at children who weren't there, telling them he knew they'd been the ones who'd TP'd his house.

By the time they'd made it back to his driveway, Adam's legs were burning, and sweat had glued his shirt to his chest. Adam deposited his companions at the steps and then stopped to catch his breath and check on his patients. Robert looked like he was clinging to life by the slimmest of threads. He'd coughed and hacked for most of the walk, leaving a trail of bright red blood behind them. Ethan was lucid again, asking for water and wanting to know how far the hospital was.

"Let me grab my keys and get you some water," Adam said. "I won't be long."

Ethan sighed and nodded, seemingly content with the brief respite on the stairs.

As he climbed the stairs to the front door, Adam took a moment to acknowledge his own fear, his own biologically programmed survival instinct. Whatever it was Terry Sanders had died of, whatever it was these two perfectly nice people had, Adam did not want to catch it. His primal self, the one lingering deep in the DNA he shared with his ancestors and their ancestors, wanted to run, wanted to leave these guys to die, and his primal self didn't feel the least bit bad about it. The fear was huge, careening through him like a wrecking ball, and he felt it growing with each passing moment. He let that part of himself have its fantasy, state its case, and then he bottled it up.

When he was in medical school, it had taken him a little while to adjust to the fact that he was going to be frequently exposed to all manner of dread illness. Then, as a first-year resident, doing a rotation in the emergency room one cold December night, he'd experienced every health-care worker's worst nightmare – an errant needle stick in the soft flesh between his left thumb and forefinger while he'd been treating an HIV-positive drug addict. He underwent the prophylactic drug treatment provided to healthcare workers who'd suffered accidental pokes and submitted to HIV tests every four weeks for a year, all of which came back negative.

Shitty as it was, the experience had made him a better physician. He knew what patients were thinking about while waiting for test results to tell them what was causing the headaches, the vaginal bleeding, the abnormal ultrasound. It expanded his reservoir of patience, something he'd been in short supply of in the first part of his residency. And since the needle stick, he'd been able to compartmentalize the fear, lock it away in a place where it couldn't overwhelm him. But he always acknowledged it. He didn't want to get sick. He didn't want to die. He was no different than anyone else. And there were times, like now, where the fear threatened to break free and paralyze him.

If Robert and Ethan had what Sanders had, then Adam had suffered two major exposures. He accepted that he was scared beyond any plane he'd ever imagined and then crammed two tons of ball-shrinking terror into a five-gallon bag. He thought about Rachel and found himself glad that she was three thousand miles away, far away from this, whatever this was.

He refocused his attention on Robert and Ethan. He took the steps two at a time, but it wasn't fast enough. When he reached the bottom of the stairs, Robert was in the throes of a massive seizure, his body flopping around the concrete driveway. Like Terry Sanders, a man he presumably had not known and would never meet, Robert DeSilva died, horribly, virtually alone, and far from home.

"Shit," Adam said to no one. "Shit, shit, shit."

He looked around for Ethan and noticed the boy

had disappeared. Christ, Adam thought, where did he go?

"Ethan?" he called out. "Son, are you there?"

He heard a soft moan coming from behind him, deeper into the carport under the house. He edged his way around his car, his heart pounding. A smear of fresh color caught his eye, toward the back corner of the driveway. Adam followed it to the shed where he stored a grill, boogie boards, half-empty paint cans, the byproducts of life of a beach house owner. It was cool and dark here. The boy was sitting cross-legged in the corner, his back against a stack of boogie boards. He looked up at Adam, a sheepish look on his face, as though he'd been caught breaking into the place.

"Ethan, it's me. My name is Adam."

"How's my dad?"

Adam didn't lie to patients, and he was not going to start now. He responded with an almost imperceptible shake of his head. Ethan leaned his head back against an old, cracked boogie board, a faded blue thing stenciled with the words Wave Destroyer in a repeating pattern down the surface of the board. The news didn't seem to affect Ethan one way or another.

"I don't suppose you knew the Sanders family?" Adam asked. "They were staying next door to my house?"

Ethan shook his head.

"We've got to get you to the hospital," Adam said. "Right now."

"What about my mom and sister?"

He coughed, a little thing that got away from him, but Adam could tell this poor kid was now in the end stages of this thing. Blood bubbled out onto the fist he'd tried to use to cut the cough off. Adam found himself thinking about Rachel again; this boy wasn't much younger than her, and that was when the fear began to break through. The box had sprung a leak. He was gripped with the urge to call her right now and tell her to run for the hills until he could get a better handle on what was precisely was going on.

"We'll call on the way," Adam said, his spirits lifted by the mere fact that he had a plan to do something. "You know their numbers, right?"

"I think so," Ethan said, carefully examining his bloodstained hand like it was an unusual seashell he'd found on the shore.

"I'm sorry," Adam said. "About your dad."

"Thanks," Ethan said. There wasn't much *oomph* in his response, a testament to how poorly Ethan was obviously feeling. Then: "Am I going to die, too?"

The question buzzed through Adam like a mild electrical shock, but he didn't answer right away. As he considered Ethan's impossible query, he helped the boy into his Explorer and they began making their way toward the causeway. A few miles east, he began to hear a car horn honking in the distance. He welcomed the sound in all its distracting familiarity. It suggested there was still order here on Holden Beach, and it gave him time to construct an appropriate response to Ethan's question.

"Let's get you some help," he said. "We'll be at the hospital soon." Adam stole another glance at Ethan, who was looking absently out at the road ahead of them.

"What's that?" he asked weakly, pointing a thin finger ahead of them.

Adam's gaze followed Ethan's finger east, and he found the source of the car horn as they approached the turn-off to the causeway, which fed back onto the mainland. But it wasn't one car horn. It was many, and it looked like a parking lot had metastasized in the middle of Ocean Boulevard. There were dozens of cars jammed together, all facing east, people honking over one another, no one moving an inch. Adam slowed to a crawl and came to a stop about a hundred yards short of the intersection. Pockets of people milled about here and there, a few smoking cigarettes, most pointing and talking.

"Wait here," Adam said. "I'm going to see what's going on."

Ethan nodded, and Adam alighted from the car, his heart pounding. It was getting hot again, the freshness of the day passing as another juicy air mass settled in on the area. Adam looked south toward water's edge, the ocean gray and lifeless. They were in the down-town area of Holden Beach, as it were, smack in the middle of a strip of real estate offices, ice cream parlors, places hawking cheap beach gear, t-shirts, hermit crabs that would be dead before their new owners made it back to Route 17. It was here vacations began and ended, the gateway from and back to real life.

Up ahead of him, a trio, two men and a woman, had gathered at the front bumper of a Honda minivan with Georgia plates. A bumper sticker on the center of the rear windshield exhorted the DAWGS to GO! The sliding doors were open, and Adam could see two small kids, strapped into their car seats in the dim passenger compartment. Both appeared to be asleep.

"What's going on?" he asked, trying to mask his growing sense of alarm. Try as he might to avoid it, his gaze kept drifting to the interior of the minivan, on the two kids sleeping in their car seats. He wondered what he would see if he drew in for a closer look, whether he'd see blood smeared across their lips like fingerpaint.

The woman and the younger man, both of whom somehow appeared flushed and pale at the same time, bright red cheeks against a backdrop of gray skin, looked at their companion, deferring to the eldest member of the group. He was in his fifties, heavy-set with a graying beard.

"Some kinda accident," the man said. He leaned in close to Adam, conspiratorially, and added: "I got a real mess here. Whole family's sick with something or the other, trying to get them to the hospital up in Shallotte."

Adam ran his fingers through his hair, thinking about Ethan DeSilva, about the empty beach, wondering if this time, the human race had run out of luck. He felt like he was living the beginning of a bad dystopian movie. He'd first felt it on the morning of the September 11 attacks, when a rumor had spread through the hospital that New York City had been nuked. He was busy with a difficult C-section and didn't get the full story until later that morning. He'd been almost relieved to discover that only a few thousand had died, as opposed to a few million, a relief he still felt guilty about more than a decade later. He'd felt it in 2008, when Lehman Brothers went down, and then Bear Stearns, one after another, and the global economy had teetered on the brink of failure and he was ready to walk down to the bank and withdraw every bit he had in cash before it went up in smoke.

"Yeah," Adam said, not knowing what else to say.

"Yeah," the man said with a disturbing hint of resignation in his voice. "My daughter and son-in-law are both sick too. I started running a fever a couple hours ago."

"Excuse me for a minute."

Adam went back to his truck to check on Ethan, out of answers, out of ideas, nearly out of his mind. The boy was slumped over in his seat, unresponsive, the seatbelt straining under Ethan's dead weight. Adam pressed two fingers against the boy's wrist, checking for the radial pulse. It was there, but thready at best.

"Have you seen anything on the news?" Adam asked when he returned to talk to the man.

"You haven't seen the news? All kinds of crazy shit. Hell, I heard one story saying all the New York Yankees had gotten sick and died. Then another story said their charter plane went down after an engine failure."

Adam stared at the man, slack-jawed.

"You're telling me this thing is everywhere?"

The man didn't respond.

Adam hadn't watched television or picked up a newspaper since he'd arrived here nearly a week ago. He pictured this thing burning through city after city, state after state, leaving graveyards in its wake. He remembered a bit of history about the Spanish flu outbreak of 1918, how that strain of influenza had spread around the world in less than a month, in an era when commercial air travel was virtually nonexistent and even automobiles were still considered a luxury item. He shuddered to think how quickly something this virulent could spread across the nation, across the globe, in this day and age. It could kill thousands of people in the blink of an eye. The idea of this kind of outbreak on a large scale threatened to turn his guts to liquid.

While Adam processed this new bit of information, his news source began coughing. It was a protracted affair, yet another incident that again left Adam feeling as helpless as he had ever felt in his life. The cough brought the man to his knees, and Adam stepped forward and placed a hand on his back. The man was baking with fever, a hellish heat that Adam was becoming far too familiar with. As the spell eased up, the man turned to the side to pat his mouth with a handkerchief. Adam appreciated the man's discretion, but there was no hiding what was happening.

Taking the hand Adam offered him, the man struggled back to his feet, one at a time.

A STORM WAS ROLLING in from the west as Adam made his way back to the cottage, having given up on the hospital. A purplish ridge of clouds was easing in, almost like a shroud over the area. Adam turned on his wipers as the fat drops of rain began spattering the salt-crusted windshield; he was briefly soothed by the familiar *wip-woop-wip-woop* of the wiper blades slicing across the glass. As the wind freshened, the skies opened up, forcing Adam to let up on the accelerator. He switched on the headlights, but they did little good against the volume of rain unleashed in the monsoon. Within seconds, his visibility had dropped to zero, and so he carefully edged over to the side of the road, more up on the sidewalk than not, and stopped in front of an undeveloped expanse of marsh.

As he braked, Ethan's failing body listed toward him, close enough that he could smell a perverse combination of Old Spice and sickness emanating from the boy. Panic surged through him like electrical spikes. More cracks were forming in his box now. He wasn't sure how much more he could take before it ruptured, like the bulkheads on Titanic after its kiss from the iceberg, before the fear got big enough to pull him under. He found himself swallowing frequently, his hands brushing against glands, on high alert for the slightest sign of infection.

Then the seizure hit. Ethan flopped around the passenger seat, his shell of a body spraying blood across the seats, the dashboard, the windshield, as if the pathogen was intent on perpetuating itself in every way possible. He wrapped his arms around the boy and held him close. The seizure was massive, powerful, a magnitude that Adam had never experienced before. It was like a bolt of lightning had dropped from the heavens and struck the boy. Adam held on for the entire duration of the seizure, refusing to let the boy die alone, tears streaming down his cheeks.

When it was over, Adam shifted back into his seat, his arms and neck splattered with blood, as if he'd just finished slaughtering a hog. Ethan was dead. Tears ran silently down Adam's cheeks, the byproduct of a hot stew of anger and fear and sadness fermenting inside him. It was like he was being made to relive that terrible day with Patient A over and over again, on a much bigger stage, the only constant being his total and complete incompetence, his inability to do one single, solitary thing to help these people.

This was off the charts, the kind of thing discussed hypothetically, maybe joked about in the CDC cafeteria. An invisible tidal wave, wiping the cities clean of life, leaving graveyard after graveyard in its viral wake until it burned itself out.

He dug his smartphone out of his pocket and tried accessing the mobile Internet application. As he waited, he noticed the squall was easing up. He checked the screen again, but it remained blank, the page still trying to load. He shifted back into gear and nosed his way back out onto Ocean Boulevard. Water had ponded in the typical lower-lying spots, and he slalomed around those dark, brooding puddles.

Back at the house, he set Ethan's body next to his father's and covered them with a tarp. Then he retreated to his bedroom with a bottle of scotch and a heavy glass tumbler, his initials etched on the side, and, for reasons he couldn't explain, locked the door behind him. A check of his watch told him it was quarter until six, almost time for the news. While he waited, he conducted another systems check. No fever, no sore throat, no nasal congestion, no unusual skin rashes or lesions, and most welcome, no swollen glands.

He started to dial his office but then remembered that it was after business hours.

He dialed Joe McCann's cell phone number.

No answer.

He dialed his friend Mark Zalewski's number.

No answer.

He dialed his old girlfriend Stephanie Hartman's number.

No answer.

He scrolled through his contacts and paused on Rachel's number for five full minutes before he could muster the courage to call her.

He dialed Rachel's number.

No answer.

He put away his phone.

INTERLUDE

BULK E-MAIL SENT TO 3.2 MILLION UNIQUE E-MAIL
ADDRESSES

From: CheapMeds@projectblue.com

Date:August 9, 20XX

To:Unidentified Recipients

Subject: MEDUSA VACCINE

DON'T BE A VICTIM!

*MEDUSA IS A DEADLY DISEASE SWEEPING THE
WORLD.*

BUT YOU CAN KEEP YOUR FAMILY SAFE

*100 EZ –SWALLOW TABLETS OF ANTIVIRAL FOR
$29.95*

DOUBLE MONEY-BACK GUARANTEE

7

"Briggs!"

Freddie turned his head toward the voice, coming from the brightly lit corridor, deep in the cinderblock bowels of the Smyrna City Jail. He'd been lying on his back on the thin bedroll, staring at the ceiling, marking time since he'd been arrested three days ago. It had been a Friday afternoon, too late for a bond hearing, and since it was a malicious wounding charge, they wouldn't let him out on his own recognizance. Due to his celebrity, the sheriff had assigned Freddie to an isolation cell, the one in which they stuck the potential suicides, rather than risk a cafeteria riot over the fact that Freddie had played for the Patriots instead of retiring with dignity as a Falcon. The cell had been sanitized of anything an inmate could use to harm himself. No sheets, no metal bed frame. Just bars, concrete, and time.

After coming to, he'd quietly followed the arresting officers (three of them!) out to the police cruiser waiting in the parking lot of the Duckling, the memory of his little bar brawl with Randy Ferguson still fresh in his mind. He shook his head when the officers asked him if he was going to give them any trouble. They all knew who he was, of course, and they appeared terrified, although he wasn't sure if that was because of his celebrity or because they were worried he might try to eat them. No, he hadn't given them any trouble; in fact, he hadn't uttered a word since the last dumb-shit thing he'd said to Ferguson before they'd done their dance. Instead, he kept asking himself the same question, over and over, wondering why he'd let that loser push his buttons the way he had.

He hadn't come up with an answer, and now, with the bond hearing done, it was time to go home and face his family. His heart began pounding, harder and harder as the footsteps drew closer, and he felt a little silly, like a little boy afraid of being punished. He took quick stock of his cell. It was a small cell, about eight-by-eight square, steeped in a pungent stew of urine and sweat and body odor. Pathetic as these environs were, and as happy as he was to be taking his leave of them, they had given him some time to think. About football, about Susan, about the future, about the next step. First, there was going to be hell to pay at home. In a strange bit of irony, nothing drove Susan bat-shit crazier than Freddie's temper. Fine, he thought. It was time to grow up. Time to be a man.

"Briggs?" the man said when he arrived. He was black, tall and thin, his posture and demeanor suggesting a stint in the military. "I'm Captain Allen Freeman. You'll be due in court on August 22 on a charge of disorderly conduct, drunk in public, and malicious wounding."

Richie Matas, Freddie's agent, trailed just behind. Matas looked pale, his thin face drawn tight, like a robe on a cold morning. This struck Briggs as odd. Matas represented a number of athletes, and this was not his first time bailing one of them out of jail. Part of the job description, he'd once commented to Freddie. Freddie stood silently, frozen by embarrassment. It wasn't the first night he'd ever spent in the clink, but it hadn't happened since his freshman year at LSU. Susan had always warned him he'd end up there again if he wasn't careful.

"I owe you one, Richie," Freddie said.

"Listen, Freddie," Matas said. "We need to get you home. Something's wrong with Susan. I drove over this morning to pick her up to come get you, and the girls said she was really sick."

"What the hell are you talking about?" Freddie asked.

Matas was walking quickly, almost jogging up the corridor to the booking area, where Freddie would be able to retrieve his personal belongings. The deputy processed Briggs out of the jail as quickly as he could, which, for Freddie, wasn't nearly quick enough. He and Matas raced back to the car and set out for the Briggs home, in a ritzy development on the north side of Smyrna.

They rode in silence, Richie unwilling or unable to relay any information other than that Susan hadn't looked good. Freddie had tried calling the house, but no one answered. About five miles out, Freddie's cell phone, which was still in his hand after he'd retrieved it from the jail inventory, began ringing.

"Dad?" a tiny voice said.

"Sweetie, it's Daddy, what's wrong?"

"It's Mom," Caroline said. Her words were choked with phlegm, as if she'd been crying.

He pinned the phone against his shoulder and tapped Matas on the right shoulder.

"Hurry up," Freddie said. "Something's wrong."

He put the phone back to his ear and took a deep breath, hoping he could stay calm, for the sake of his hysterical daughter. "What is it, sweetie?"

"She lay down on the couch for a bit, said she was

too tired to get upstairs," Caroline said, her voice cracking. "Then she started coughing, and there's blood everywhere." Now each of Heather's words was punctuated with a sobbing heave.

"Caroline, listen to me very carefully. Stay with her," Freddie said. "I'm calling an ambulance."

Freddie killed the line and called 911. Strangely, it took three tries to get through.

The line clicked open, and Freddie started to speak when he was interrupted by a recorded message.

"Thank you for calling the City of Smyrna's Emergency Operations Center. All of our dispatchers are busy assisting other citizens. Please stay on the line, and your call will be taken in the order it was received."

"What the fuck is this shit?" Freddie bellowed, as the message began to replay.

"What?" Matas asked.

Freddie pulled the phone away from his ear and pressed the speakerphone button.

"-on the line, and your call will be taken in the order it was received."

It began to replay again.

"What the hell?" Matas said.

"Put on hold by 911?" Freddie said, looking over at Matas.

Matas shrugged and pushed down on the gas, determined to get them back to the Briggs house as fast as possible. As they hurtled north around Smyrna, they heard the message twice more in its entirety and most of a third time before a dispatcher came on the line.

"911, what is your emergency?" a gruff voice barked at him.

He told the dispatcher what he knew.

"I'll dispatch an EMS crew, sir, but you should be aware we've had an unusually high call volume this morning."

Freddie tried to say something, but the words weren't there. He looked over at Matas, his hands spread apart, unsure of what to do.

"Just send the fucking ambulance!" Matas barked into the phone.

"Thanks," Freddie said, hanging up.

"Fuck it," Matas said. "If the ambulance isn't there, we'll take her ourselves."

Freddie nodded, the panic rising, filling him like a balloon and making it difficult to breathe. Richie Matas, God bless him, pushed down the gas pedal of his rented Audi as far as it would go, determined to make the ten-minute drive home in three. The jail was in the southern part of Smyrna, in a beaten-down industrial area about as far as one could get from the northern suburbs where Freddie and Susan had made their home and still be in Smyrna. Freddie and Susan had bought the six-thousand-square-foot home about a year into his career, after they'd gotten used to the idea of having millions of dollars in the bank, gotten used to the idea of not ever having to worry about money again.

Freddie and Susan had both come up poor, and they'd never forgotten the pain of growing up in Smyrna's trailer parks, which was where they'd first met more than a dozen years earlier. They were scrupulous savers. Freddie loved teasing her for clipping coupons on Sunday mornings, which she said she did to keep her mind off the game, worried sick as she was of watching him end up paralyzed or worse. The house was their sole extravagance. They wanted a place that would be home forever, where they would raise their girls, twelve-year-old Caroline, and Heather, a month shy of her eighth birthday. They wanted a place where they could grow old with the neighbors, where they could take refuge, a sanctuary away from the madness accompanying life as an NFL superstar.

A few minutes later, the turn-off into Freddie's subdivision came into view. As Matas slowed to turn onto the private drive feeding into the subdivision, Freddie heard the ambulance screaming toward him.

"Quick, get up to the guardhouse," he said to Matas.

A moment later, the ambulance appeared in his rearview mirror, screaming its frantic howl. The guard waved them through, and the ambulance rumbled down the wide avenue, now less than a mile from its destination. Matas fell in behind the ambulance, close enough to cross that line from tailgating to drafting, fully flaunting the admonition that he should "Keep Back 500 Feet."

They covered the mile in about forty-five seconds. The ambulance slowed briefly, dipping right into the Briggs' semi-circular driveway, and then came to a halting stop at its midpoint. Matas lagged behind a couple car lengths and met the crew at the ambulance's back door. Two paramedics, a young woman with close-cut blonde hair and a tall heavy-set black guy, got to work unloading their gear. Freddie recognized the man as a teacher at Caroline's school. Mr. Rowe or something like that. He must have been a part-time EMT. Both were wearing powder-blue surgical masks. A handful of neighbors milled about, gathered in small clumps, whispering, pointing.

"Please hurry," Freddie croaked as he met the paramedics.

They ignored him as they unloaded the stretcher and their gear from the back of the truck. As he passed the open doors of the ambulance bay, Freddie realized with horror that four other people were in the back, looking flushed, looking very sick. He put them out of his mind and led them inside. As he made his way down the corridor, he heard Susan coughing, a deep, guttural, hacking cough. He'd never heard anything like it in his life.

"Susan? Girls?"

No response.

"Susan!"

He turned the corner beyond the sunken living room and stepped into the galley-style kitchen, where his shoe slipped out underneath him. His big frame crashed to the floor, and he felt a sharp pain shoot through his right knee. Oh, no, he thought. Thoughts of all the time he'd spent rehabbing the knee came roaring up inside him, followed by a scorching chaser of guilt. He rolled over on his side and started to push himself up on the fresh, bright-red blood slicking the floor. He scampered to his feet, panic engulfing him like fire consuming a house. Freddie heard a female voice behind him, startling him. He'd almost forgotten the paramedics were there.

"Look," the woman paramedic – Gibert, according to the ID card clipped to her breast pocket – was saying. Freddie, panic-stupid now, saw her pointing at something, and he followed her index finger to the back of the kitchen, just beyond the Viking refrigerator.

"What's in there?" Gibert asked, pointing toward a closed door.

"Mudroom," Freddie said as the pair rushed

forward, Freddie close behind. "Leave the stretcher out here. It's pretty tight in there."

"Oh shit!" said Rowe, the first one in the door. "In here!"

He slipped into the mudroom behind them, desperate to see her but careful not to interfere with their provision of care. He was a good six inches taller than Rowe, more than a foot clear of Gibert, so he was able to see what was going on. His stomach clenched as he saw the amount of blood splattered on the walls, puddled on the floor. Susan was on her side, curled up into a ball, facing the wall. At first, Freddie thought she was dead, but he saw her shift her right foot, and he felt tears well up in his eyes.

"Aw shit," Rowe said, mostly to himself. "What the hell is this shit?"

"Shut up," Gibert hissed. "Roll her over. We need to get her out of here."

She turned her head to address Freddie. "Sir, is anyone else in the house feeling sick?"

"I don't know. I don't think so."

The girls. Where were the girls? He slipped back down the corridor to the staircase and took the steps two at a time. He was sweating badly, and he could smell a strange odor emanating from his body, a whisky-tinted, fear-coated musk. It felt hot in the house, too hot, even though he could hear the soft, reassuring hiss of the air conditioning blowing through the vents. As he approached the closed door of the media room, he heard a sound that severed his connection with reality. His mind was trapped in a netherworld between the three corners of panic, terror, and anger.

It was a terrible sound. A horrible, ripping sound.

His daughter Caroline was coughing.

INTERLUDE

TRANSCRIPT OF VIDEO UPLOADED AUGUST 10

3.4 Million Hits Before Video was Removed

Shaky video of parking lot. Image blurs and then is obscured by videographer's hand

"Um, I'm standing about a block north of Turner Field here in Atlanta. That there is the west parking lot of the stadium. There's been a lot of military activity all morning. I don't know... wait, people are unloading from the back of the convoy trucks. I don't know ... [COUGHING SPELL] lining them up. [WHEEZY BREATHING] Been hearing rumors of a vaccine. I woke up with it, whatever it is. I feel pretty good overall, maybe I got a mild case or something."

[SOUND OF MACHINE GUN FIRE]

"Holy fucking shit! The soldiers, they just opened up on those poor people! Oh my God, this can't be happening. This can't be happening!"

[WHIMPERS]

"I'm going to try and get a little bit closer."
Video becomes blurry and shaky
"Jesus. [inaudible]. Oh, Jesus, Jesus."
[SOUND OF MACHINE GUN FIRE]
"Oh, shit. I gotta upload this shit."
[SOUND OF COUGHING]
[VIDEO ENDS]

8

"You know, Kevin," Kevin Butler said to his empty office, just a stone's throw from the Oval Office, "you probably should've listened to that guy Ponce."

Then a coughing spell. Hard, ab-shredding coughing.

"No, we should've nuked the Bronx!" he said. Then he laughed.

He took off his dress shirt, leaving him in a white t-shirt and Joseph Abboud pants. He didn't know why he did it. It just seemed like a good idea. When he was done, he sat back down to rest because the simple act of removing his shirt had left him spent. He sat there in his white t-shirt and sweat-soaked Joseph Abboud pants. Or maybe it was piss. He didn't know anymore.

God, he felt like shit.

He cried for a few minutes. Then he stopped because he forgot what he was crying about. Then he remembered he was crying because he was dying, but he didn't start crying again because it required a tincture of effort that he did not currently possess.

He looked at the clock on the mantel. It was three-thirty in the afternoon. He didn't know if his family was alive or dead. He had no idea what day it was, but he didn't really care. All the days had piled up on top of one another, a big car crash of blocks on a calendar. They were all the same day now.

How had he gotten here?

You walked, a little voice called out.

He laughed the manic laugh of a man whose links to reality were breaking, one at a time.

No, not here here. *HERE.*

Oh, HERE.

He thought about the path that had led him *HERE*, about the million tiny decisions he'd made and forgotten, and the million tiny events he'd had no control over, the way those things had braided themselves together into the tapestry that was Kevin Butler's life. He thought he'd figured it out, where it had all begun nearly thirty years ago, an unseasonably warm January morning during his final year of law school at Harvard. Around dawn, he'd been jolted from sleep by a strange noise and had been stunned to see an intruder in his bedroom (his bedroom!), rifling through the drawers of his bureau, looking for God knew what. And only God had known what that man had been looking for, because upon noticing Butler was awake, the burglar had fled the crappy apartment in the crappy neighborhood, never to be seen again.

Butler looked down at his hands, thinking about his law school burglar for the first time in decades, manic-eyed and mangy, so dirty Butler hadn't been able to tell if he was black or white. The experience had convinced him to abandon corporate law and sent him down a much different path, starting as an assistant district attorney in Texas, where he took special joy in prosecuting home invaders, through the state Attorney General's office, to the U.S. Senate, before his old buddy Nathan Crosby, then the governor of Oklahoma, had tapped him to serve as his campaign manager for a presidential run.

The campaign, dismissed in the early days by the pundits as a wild hair, had taken off like wildfire, starting with an unexpectedly strong showing in Iowa, followed by a huge influx of cash to float them through the early primaries. Success begat success, and they'd secured the nomination in Los Angeles that summer, neither of them really believing it was happening until Crosby had taken a concession phone call from the man he'd defeated in the general election, the unpopular Democratic incumbent who'd presided over an economic collapse and had been unable to accomplish just about anything.

When you got right down to it, it had been that anonymous thief who'd shoved Kevin Butler toward his destiny, toward this moment in the White House, struggling (and failing) to deal with the biggest crisis the nation had ever faced. If it hadn't been for that burglar, if he'd rented a different apartment the previous August, if he'd spent the night at his then-girlfriend's place, which he hadn't because they'd had a big fight, if one of a million other things had broken differently, he'd probably have never changed his career track. He'd be a partner at some big firm in D.C. or Chicago or New York, living in some gated community, growing increasingly worried at the widening epidemic.

He didn't know where the President was.

He didn't even know if the man was alive.

His phone rang. It was probably someone very important bearing some very important news that would be very bad, and so he didn't answer it. Ooh, wait, let me guess!

A quarantine broke in Dallas!

No, no, wait! Let me guess! Riots in Des Moines!

Or Army units in Boston are abandoning their posts!

It had all come apart, and he was so, so afraid.

He was burning up now, the sweat pouring off him in rivers.

It had been nearly a week since Medusa had first appeared on their radar. There had been no communication with either the CDC or USAMRIID in at least a day, and he didn't expect any more. Not that they could offer anything more than what they already knew. It was sort of an academic exercise at this point. Under the microscope, the virus bore close resemblance to a snake, similar in structure to the Ebola and Marburg viruses, *blah, blah, blah*. But for all its similarities to those two scary pathogens, plenty scary in their own right, Medusa was different, so achingly and astonishingly different.

The thing that had driven the doctors out of their minds, right up until it killed them, was that they didn't know how it was different. Why was it spreading so rapidly? Why was it airborne? Why was it killing so quickly? Even Ebola Zaire, the deadliest pathogen known to man (until last week, that is), took days to kill its host. They hadn't even had time to figure out where Medusa had come from. And now they would never know! Atlanta was gone. Fort Detrick was gone. Despite all their precautions, Medusa had wiped out both installations.

What surprised Butler the most was how incompetent he'd felt, how foolish, how stupid, and he was one of the ones that was supposed to figure out how they were going to stop this goddamn thing! It had always been a source of amusement that the world often turned on things he said and did and things he told the President to say and do. He still felt like they were playing grownup, like it was Model U.N. or Student Council, and that certainly, the real grownups would swoop in and take over and fix everything. And the fear. He couldn't believe how scared he was.

He stepped out into the hallway outside his office. The lights were on, everything running normally, but it was dead quiet. He'd never heard it so quiet in his three years working here. There was a body in the corridor, one of his staffers, Julie or Donna. He couldn't remember her name. She was single, childless, and had stuck it out here, "managing the crisis," as they had called it. Many others had fled.

He coughed hard, spraying blood across the wall. He poked his head in the office of one of his deputies, but it was empty. Office after office he visited, staggering from one to the next, using the wall to support himself. This was one was empty, that one contained a body. It became a bit of a game. Empty Office, 2, Dead Body, 1. Ooh, and now it's tied. Two apiece!

He was getting tired now.

He found a break room and sat at one of the tables. Before him, the vending machines hummed along, the soda ice cold, the snack cakes fresh and moist. And they would stay that way, long after Kevin Butler died. Even if humanity had succeeded in erasing itself from the hard drive, the lights would stay on here. The White House might someday go dark, but it wouldn't be any time soon. Maybe ten years from now. Maybe a hundred.

"OK," he said to no one.

He bowed his head and recited the Lord's Prayer. It felt phony and forced because reciting the Lord's Prayer was pretty fucking vanilla when you got down to it, like you weren't even trying, like you were just going through the motions. Kevin had once fervently believed in God, and the Butlers had been a church-going family, because you didn't become the Chief of Staff to a Republican president without the appropriate set pieces on the stage of your life. Over the years, though, his faith had grown weaker, like a radio station getting farther and farther away with each passing mile, its signal breaking up, heavily laced with static.

"... for thine is the Kingdom, the power and the glory, forever and ever, Amen."

Butler opened his eyes and found a young staffer staring at him. Her nose and mouth, caked with blood. Copies of copies of copies. It started to get old after a while. *I get it, God, I fucked up!* I should've agreed to the quarantine or paid a little more attention to that intelligence briefing about that bioterrorist group in Waco or whatever it was that we missed that had brought us to this point.

"Hi," he thought he said to the young woman, but it actually came out, "Heaaagghhhh!"

The staffer turned and fled down the corridor.

Kevin bought a bag of potato chips and sat back down to eat them. They did not agree with him and he vomited violently on the floor of the break room.

He laid his head down on the table and died at four-thirty that afternoon.

FROM THE STATE NEWSPAPER (COLUMBIA, SOUTH CAROLINA)

EXTRA!
SOUTH CAROLINA SECEDES FROM UNION
WASHINGTON THREATENS NEW REPUBLIC

By SIOBHAN MOON

The State Staff Writer

COLUMBIA (August 13) – Calling the Medusa virus an "unprecedented" threat to its continued existence, the state of South Carolina officially seceded from the United States of America last night for the second time in its history, renaming itself the People's Republic of Columbia and installing former Governor Alan Moran as its new President.

"The people of this brave new nation have spoken," said President Moran, speaking from an undisclosed location. "This towering crisis has forced us to make some difficult decisions, and we believe that we alone hold the key to our survival. The government of the United States has proven itself unable to handle this catastrophe, and we will not stand idly by while my fellow citizens suffer."

The secession became official at 11:18 p.m. last night, when then-Governor Moran placed his signature on the state's Declaration of Secession, which had been passed unanimously in both houses of the South Carolina legislature earlier that evening.

The House of Representatives voted 44-0 in favor of secession, with 80 House members unable to participate due to illness. The South Carolina Senate quickly followed suit, unanimously passing the resolution 14-0, with 32 senators abstaining due to illness.

Moran added that the borders of his nation were closed indefinitely, and that any unauthorized persons attempting to enter Columbia would be dealt with "harshly and swiftly."

The White House reacted angrily, quickly issuing a statement denouncing the secession and threatening military action to preserve the Union.

"The United States does not recognize the so-called 'sovereignty' of the state of South Carolina," the statement said. "This White House is confident the state's action is a legal nullity and has no effect. Furthermore, this Administration considers Governor Moran and his 58 state legislators to be traitors, and they will be held accountable for this ridiculous act. The U.S. does not acknowledge Governor Moran's so-called borders, and any attempt by the state of South Carolina to enforce those borders will be met with force."

The current status of the state's nine military bases was unknown at press time.

According to multiple sources, several other states are considering similar secession resolutions, including Virginia, North Carolina, and Tennessee.

9

A steady rain fell as Adam crossed the James River just south of the Richmond city limits on that Friday evening, the thirteenth of August. Spires of frozen traffic stretched away in either direction along I-95, and in the distance, he counted three fires burning against the backdrop of downtown. The lights of the cityscape shined dully against the twilight, but at least they were still on, a fact that Adam was deeply grateful for. He checked his watch; it was just past seven-thirty. He was drenched, exhausted, and starving. The one thing he was not, to his pure and utter amazement, was sick. Physically, he felt perfectly fine. The country appeared to be crumbling around him under the weight of this invisible conqueror, which had, so far, overlooked him.

And somehow, that made it worse.

The waiting.

It had been one week since he'd first encountered what the media were now calling the Medusa virus, and based on the few bits and pieces he'd been able to cobble together, the virus was burning its way across the globe and order was starting to break down. And Medusa's communicability was like nothing ever seen or studied. After the deaths of the DeSilvas (and he never had found the remaining family members), he'd spent two days on Holden Beach trying to tend to sick vacationers, trying something, anything to keep someone alive. And all he had seen had left him terrified, hopeless, adrift.

He'd tended to the bodies of the DeSilva men the morning after they died. It took an hour, but he finally had gotten them indoors, lying side by side on his kitchen floor, covered with sheets, perhaps a fraction of their dignity preserved. Adam had tackled the senior DeSilva first, a job that had all but wiped him out. Ethan's father had outweighed Adam by fifty pounds, and so Adam had dragged him up the staircase, his arms locked around the big man's chest. One step at a time Adam had taken, his arms and back burning with liquid fire. At one point, just two from the top step, Adam had gotten a little off balance, a little high on the rain-slicked stairs, and he'd nearly lost his purchase; he felt both of them teetering downward, a tumble that Adam feared would leave him as dead as the DeSilvas. He managed to find his seat before he fell forward, slamming his tailbone down against the wet edge of the step. After a quick rest, he finished the job, and he brought Robert to what, unbeknownst to Adam, would in fact become his and his son's final resting place.

Adam made shorter work of Ethan's remains. The boy had been tall but rail-thin, a body that would never fill out. As Adam hoisted him over his shoulder, he felt the boy's smooth cheek rub against his own; it was a face that hadn't seen the edge of a razor yet. Adam was reminded of Ethan's youth, of all the promise that would go unfulfilled, and an immense sadness swept through him. He thought about all the things Ethan DeSilva would never do, never see, and he felt his eyes water like a heavy cloud. Maybe he was being a bit maudlin, because for all Adam knew, Ethan might have grown up to be an embezzler or a drug dealer or child molester, but he didn't want to think about that right now. Whatever possible future may have lain ahead, Ethan DeSilva deserved a better fate than he had gotten.

Standing in his kitchen among dead men, Adam's muscles ached and his legs quivered with exhaustion. He searched for something to say to the DeSilvas, some eloquent benediction to bid them farewell from this world, but he could think of nothing. He clicked his teeth together for a few moments.

"I'm sorry," Adam had finally said, his voice catching.

Sharp swords of guilt and regret buried themselves into Adam's soul, up to the hilt. He wished he could give them a proper funeral, but storing them inside was the best Adam could do. He wasn't planning to stay long anyway – he could simply crank up the air conditioning to help slow the rate of decomposition. For all Adam knew to the contrary, he might be joining these men in death in a day or two anyway. A sudden burst of terror then, like a kick in the stomach, and he found himself trying to imagine the DeSilvas' final moments. How afraid had they been? Did they know the end was near? Could they feel life slipping away, like the taste of something delicious dissolving into nothingness? Was it stinking, bowel-loosening terror? He thought these things, and he couldn't stop himself.

That afternoon, as he'd peered out over the ocean from the Holden Beach pier, he'd met an older Asian woman, on holiday with her family, who, like him, had remained healthy. She spoke very little English, but at some primal level, she grasped that Adam wasn't sick either. She dragged him by the collar of his shirt, all one hundred pounds of her, to her family's beach cottage. Her entire family had come down with it. The first three to fall ill, two adults and a ten-year-old girl, had already died, and the others were deteriorating rapidly. She was hysterical.

And so he waited with the elderly woman, whose name he finally learned was Sang-mi, as her beloved relatives expired, one by one, as her family disintegrated, a great machine failing unexpectedly when only hours before it had been humming along in perfect synergy and harmony.

At the goddamn beach.

He held her hand and cried with her.

Sang-mi had been inconsolable. When Adam went to pull a sheet over the body of her son, who'd been the last one to die, she bolted out the back door and onto the back deck, screaming hysterically. He raced out after her, reaching out to pull her down before she could jump, even grabbing a swatch of fabric from her peach-colored housecoat, but she was fiercely determined to join her departed relatives, and that was precisely what she had done. Sang-mi flung herself from the railing; Adam closed his eyes as she plunged down, a second later, he heard her body hit the roof of their Dodge Durango some fifty feet below, the sharp crunch of the metal skin of the roof crumpling under Sang-mi's weight.

And much like he couldn't leave the DeSilva men alone in the carport, he couldn't leave Sang-mi there, like a fragile bird that had fallen from flight, and so he carried her broken little body back upstairs and laid her to rest with the rest of her family.

He sat there with the dead family and watched the

news, and that was when it had hit home for Adam, that this monster was roaming the countryside, all the countrysides, it was everywhere and nowhere, ghostly and very real. Regular programming had been interrupted for round-the-clock news coverage of the epidemic. Outbreaks had been reported in twenty-five states and across the globe. The more he watched, the sicker he felt, hope sluicing away, like tiny grains of sand trickling through an hourglass.

Driving off the island was no longer an option; the traffic jam he'd encountered with Ethan had metastasized into a bizarre still frame of a demolition derby, cars turned every which way, smashed up against one another. So he'd ridden his bike, an old beach cruiser he kept under the house, across the causeway on the morning of the eleventh. He rode all day, stopping only to relieve himself. He made it to Wilmington at dusk, but there was no respite there, just more chaos. Large crowds drifted through the streets, loud and panicky. Automatic gunfire chattered in the twilight. It was too dark to keep riding, so he spent a restless night in an alleyway.

He had to get home.

West of Wilmington, the congestion had eased up some, enough to warrant commandeering a Ford Taurus he found by the side of the road, its driver dead of Medusa. After laying the body on the shoulder, he loaded his bike in the back seat and shoved off, sticking to the back roads cutting through central North Carolina and into Virginia. Even in these rural areas, he saw nothing but chaos. Fires burning, car wrecks, throngs of people migrating on foot, carrying what they could. He listened to the radio for news, but it was confusing and contradictory, and so he had shut it off.

By the following morning, August 13, he was about a hundred miles from home, and he decided to make the rest of the trip on the bike. Dead traffic choked I-95, so he had used the cars as refueling stations, raiding them for snacks and water. Most of the vehicles were abandoned, but many contained the bodies of Medusa victims, their desperate flight from the plague now over.

He called Rachel half a dozen times, but on the few occasions the call went through, he got only her voice mail. Thinking about what was going on around him was too much to contemplate, and so he had simply focused on the road ahead. Terror powered his legs; his mind had shut down, perhaps as an act of self-preservation. He rode past the towns of Emporia and Jarratt and Carson and found things just as fucked up in Virginia as they'd been in North Carolina.

That had brought him here, just north of the bridge spanning the James. Adam curled onto the Broad Street exit, desperate to get home, numb, exhausted. His ass hurt from so many miles on the bike. As he merged onto Broad Street and cycled past the Virginia Commonwealth University Hospital, three gunshots cracked the night air in quick succession, one after the other – POW! POW! POW! A chilling scream followed, a howl so primal that Adam slammed down the bicycle's brakes, almost reflexively. The wheels locked up, but on the wet surface, they continued to slide underneath him; a second later, his weight disrupted the balance of the bike, tipping it over and dumping him onto the blacktop. His body rolled into the curb like a discarded beer bottle.

He lay still for a moment, anxious for reports from his various body parts. Pain buzzed through his body, but he took solace in the fact that he could feel pain everywhere. Carefully, he wiggled all the wiggly parts, starting with his feet and moving upward to his head. It was going to hurt like hell the next day, assuming he lived that long.

There were more people here, pockets of them, wandering the streets, the air buzzing with panicked voices. The tinkle of breaking glass. They were right, the novelists and screenwriters with their depictions of the apocalypse. They'd been so goddamned right. The crowd consisted mostly of young people, some of them engaged in a kind of protest march.

TRUTH NOW! one sign read.

Another: NO MORE LIES!

A third: MEDUSA IS OUR DOOM

He heard a low growl approaching from the east; a moment later, a pair of olive-green military transports pulled up and blocked the intersection at 10th and Broad Street, just a few blocks from the state capitol building.

"Clear the streets and return to your homes," a soldier announced via megaphone. "You are in violation of a military curfew."

Adam's stomach flipped. How was this happening, how was this happening, how was this happening? His feet felt locked in concrete as he watched the protestors ignore the soldiers' mandate. He could hear coughing and sneezing and if they had it, Adam thought, they really didn't have anything to lose by ignoring the soldiers. That made for a very bad combination.

He needed to get out of here.

He was half a block shy of the hospital's emergency room entrance. In the falling darkness, the familiar red lights of an ambulance strobed across the neighboring buildings. Almost instinctively, his feet began shuffling toward the door, the hospital's gravity pulling him in, his life so inextricably tied to medicine and the healing arts that there was no separating him from it, especially in the face of this immense disaster. Hell, maybe he could help out!

The closer he got, the faster he moved. He had to see for himself. One last light of hope flickered deep in his soul, perhaps nothing more than a pilot light, but, with the right spark, could reignite his faith that it wasn't as bad as it seemed, that this outbreak had burned hot and fast but like a falling star scraping the roof of the world, was flaming out, that his colleagues, his brothers and sisters in arms, were bringing their best game in their most desperate hour.

These were the thoughts pinballing around his head as he drew closer to the double doors, and these were the ones that died the most brutal deaths when he saw the words GOODNIGHT MOON grotesquely scribbled on the glass doors in ... Jesus God, was that *blood*? The sliding doors were malfunctioning, opening and closing like a metronome. To his left was the ambulance whose lights he'd seen flashing earlier; one of the bay doors was open, swaying in the rain-freshened breeze. Half a dozen bodies were piled up inside the ambulance bay.

As he drew close enough to see inside the hospital, to see the stretchers scattered about the unit like a child's abandoned toys, the smell hit him like a runaway truck. It was rich and deep, a pungent, gassy smell that all but wrapped its invisible hands around Adam's throat. He recoiled, losing his balance and finding his seat on the wet asphalt behind him. He sat in the puddle, feeling the cold rainwater seeping through his clothes, thinking about Rachel, Rachel, Rachel.

Behind him, back on the street, the protestors were growing louder. At first, he couldn't quite make out their words, a tri-syllabic chant, but as he primed his ears, the words came through loud and clear.

"Fuck you, pigs! FUCK YOU PIGS!"

Over and over they screamed it, louder and louder until the desperate chatter of gunfire exploded and cut the mantra short. Then their screams of protest were replaced by howls of pain and agony. He heard footsteps, and terror stabbed at his core.

"FUCK YOU, PIGS!"

Hide, you moron, hide!

The dark cave of the ambulance bay beckoned him; he didn't want to get in, but he had to. He grabbed the edge of the door and hoisted himself up onto the bumper. Even with the doors open, it was rank and hot, like an ancient evil expelling its hot breath on him. The sound of automatic gunfire erupted again, this time closer, much closer, almost like it was in his head, and he forced himself deeper into the ambulance, toward the back, using the dozen bodies for cover.

It was dark, but not pitch black, and that was horrible in its own way. Silhouettes moving about, soldiers pursuing and cutting down fleeing protestors, the tongues of flame erupting from the muzzles of their heavy guns.

Finally, silence, as the soldiers finished their sweep,

leaving Adam alone in the back of that dead ambulance.

Rachel, Rachel, Rachel.

Then the bad thoughts started rushing in, pouring in as if a water main had ruptured. Fear that she wouldn't answer if he called. Fear that she was already gone. Fear that he would never see her again, and he would never get a chance to make right what had gone so terribly wrong.

He had tried to make a go of it with Nina Kershaw, Rachel's mother, when they'd discovered she was pregnant. They'd been on a few dates together, so it wasn't quite a one-night stand that had led to the pregnancy. A couple weeks after the pregnancy test came back positive, they'd ridden down I-64 to Busch Gardens in Williamsburg, about an hour southeast of Richmond, just to get their minds off the very sudden and unexpected detonation of a reality bomb in their lives.

It had been a beautiful September day, the day clear and fresh with just a hint of fall in the air. They ate funnel cakes and chili dogs, and Adam had ridden the Loch Ness Monster; Nina had opted for the less exciting rides in her delicate condition. Toward the end of the day, he'd won her a gigantic stuffed bear at one of the carnival games, a stuffed animal that had stood guard over Rachel's room to this day.

On the drive back to Richmond, they'd held hands. That night, she stayed with him at his apartment, where they made love. They slept until noon, and Adam felt like everything was going to be all right. Maybe things weren't as clean or neat as he once imagined they'd be, but if there was one thing he'd learned in medical school, it was that life wasn't particularly interested in neat and clean. It was dirty and messy and sloppy, and you had to be able to adjust to it, to read the defenses, call the audibles.

And so when she had ended things three months later, there in the parking lot of St. Mary's Hospital, after the twenty-week ultrasound that had told them it was a girl, he felt like he'd been punched in the stomach. He'd missed the signs, the ground shifting underneath him, the chill in the air, the distance growing between them, two tectonic plates drifting apart.

He pulled out his phone, the glow from the screen illuminating the corpses around him. In the top left corner of the bright screen, two bars reflecting signal strength flickered at him. This worried him; he normally got great reception downtown. It was too creepy, too symbolic. Pushing the thought out of his head, he dialed her number, his heart pounding, the blood rushing in his ears.

The phone rang and rang and rang, its buzz as lonely a sound as he had ever heard in his life.

No one answered, and the call rolled into voice mail.

"Rachel, it's Dad," he said, trying to hold his panic

down like a runaway steer. "Call me. I'm not sick, but I don't know what's going on. Today is, uh..."

He had no idea what day it was. Urgent requests for information skittered along his neurons, tapping his brain for the information, but the answer was not forthcoming.

"Shit, I don't even know what day it is. Please, chicken wing, call me."

He ended the call and slipped the phone back into his pocket.

Chicken wing. That had been his nickname for her when she was a kid, a skinny mess of arms and legs. It had been years since he'd called her that.

As he retrieved his bike, two camouflaged Army trucks rolled by, headed east on Broad Street.

He had never felt so alone.

THE STORM GREW STRONGER as Adam drew closer to his house, there just near the end of Floyd Avenue. Old oaks and maples dating back to the Civil War swayed in the stiffening wind like angry sentinels. Sheets of rain washed across the blacktop, the throaty ripple of thousands of gallons of water rushing into the city's ancient storm drains audible above the downpour. Lights were still shining in many houses, the rooms bright in the falling gloom; he paused at one bay window and peered inside, cupping his hands around his eyes to sluice away the rain. He hoped, no, he prayed to see signs of life, someone watching television, lingering in front of a bookcase, making dinner. But instead, he saw a middle-aged woman on a couch, curled up under a blanket, the blue light of a television screen flickering against her face. Her eyes were closed. He moved on.

At the last intersection, he saw two people arguing, their arms wild and animated in their accusatory slashes. In the intersection, a Jeep's front quarter panel was smashed to hell, and its assailant, a large Buick sedan, now sported a crumpled front grill. Steam curled from cracked radiators.

Then the larger of the men, a heavyset, balding fellow wearing a black windbreaker, shoved the other man in the chest. The skinnier fellow stumbled backwards, and Adam's face tightened as he sensed, deep in his soul, something extraordinarily bad was about to happen. He slowed to a stop, keeping one foot perched upon the pedal, the high one, just like he'd learned as a kid. He debated making a U-turn, approaching his house via one of the other streets that-

BLAMM!

The sound of the gunshot exploded through the rain, the impact of the bullet spinning the heavyset man's body around before he crashed to the wet pavement in a heap. Adam's medical training kicked in, and he got off the bike, ready to rush to the man's side to treat the wound. Part of him wanted to be there for him, maybe give him a chance to help someone this week, after the catastrophic few days he'd spent at Holden Beach. But then that, too, was stolen from him, when the shooter stepped forward and fired two more bullets into his victim's face.

"No!" Adam called out.

The shooter looked up in Adam's direction. Their eyes locked, and in that moment, Adam saw the panic and the fear and total disintegration of everything this man might have been yesterday, hell, five minutes ago. He aimed the gun at Adam, who froze. His mind went blank; it didn't seem real, what was happening, as though he might have been watching this scene unfold on television.

Everything became exquisitely clear, down to the fat drops of rainwater forming on the barrel of the gun and then splashing down onto the blacktop to join the thin rivulets flowing across the blacktop. As Adam sat there, straddling his bicycle, the shooter held up a free hand, a defensive posture, as if he were the one facing the barrel of the gun. Then he fired.

The bullet missed by a country mile, but it sent Adam tumbling to the asphalt, pulling the bike down on top of him. His foot became tangled in the spokes of the rear tire and as he attempted to wrestle it free, he noticed the man approaching, his gun up again.

The spike of terror was so sharp Adam gagged; he kept one eye on the armed man and worked to free himself. Why hadn't he just pedaled away? He would've been three blocks away by now.

"Are you sick?" the man was yelling. "Are you sick?"

"No!" Adam called out. "Don't shoot, please don't shoot!"

Adam hoped this would defuse the situation, assure the man he had nothing to fear.

But instead, the man fired again. Adam screamed as that infernal spoke finally released his foot from captivity, but again the man had missed. He was a foot away now, close enough Adam could see the man's flushed cheeks, feel the terrible heat radiating from his rotting body.

"Why aren't you sick?"

The man stood there, unsteady on his feet, as if the street was rippling beneath him, the gun tottering from side to side. He was at point-blank range; there was nowhere for Adam to go.

"Why ... aren't... you... sick?"

Then a coughing spell overcame him, and for a moment, Adam couldn't believe his luck; he stood there, watching Medusa tear this man apart from the inside out. Finally, he made his move. He drove into the man's midsection, shoulder-first, and the pair flopped to the ground in a tangle of arms and legs. Still coughing, the man pawed at Adam's face and head, but he got up a little high, and Adam slid his hand onto the barrel of the gun. Now he had the leverage, and he began pushing the muzzle away from his torso. Next, he went for the trigger, wedging his thumb under the other man's finger into the trigger guard; he felt the skin from his knuckle peel back.

The pain was huge and immediate, like his thumb had been dipped in fire. But he dug deeper, seeking the leverage he needed now that the muzzle was facing the other way.

Dig, dig, dig, dig!

Tears streamed from the corner of his eyes and down into his ears. Every muscle howled with pain and fatigue. He felt congestion fill his nose and throat. As his left thumb continued its quest, Adam used his right arm to block the man's forehead. His lips were peeled back, his teeth flashing and clicking together. No words were exchanged, just a series of painful, desperate, primal grunts from both men.

Now or never, Adam, now or never. Adam pulled hard on the trigger, screaming like a banshee as he did so; the gun roared and bucked between their bodies. Immediately, the man's body went limp and eased down on Adam like a sigh. Adam reacted with a half-gasp, half-scream. As quickly as it had begun, it was over, and Adam was alone on the street, in the middle of this deepening shitstorm.

He staggered to his feet and stumbled in a little semi-circle around the man.

He heard himself howling, a deep, guttural thing of victory, a war cry of sorts, and he could scarcely believe the sound was coming out of his own body. He began shivering, and his stomach heaved.

Ingrained habits died hard, and so he glanced up and down the street for rubberneckers, eyewitnesses, police officers. At a house just catty-corner to him, there was a little girl standing on a covered porch, wearing a bright red dress that was emblazoned with yellow flowers. She stood there holding a stuffed pig, a blank look on her face. As Adam watched her watching him, he could hear in the distance the sounds of sirens and gunfire and shouts and screams. He looked back toward the intersection where this had all started; the two cars were still engaged in their embrace, where, unbeknownst to Adam, they would remain until the rubber tires disintegrated into dust, until the cars' metallic paint had decayed to a rusted orange.

His head hurt.

He sat down.

Right on the street.

Next to the man he'd just killed.

His mind was an empty thing, a blank notebook.

He looked back at the porch, but the little girl was gone, and he didn't know if she'd been there at all or if he'd been hallucinating. He mounted his bike again and pedaled for home. The rain intensified as he drew closer to his house, drowning out everything else. Two minutes later, he braked at his front stoop, hopped off the bike and carried it inside. His clothes were soaked with a thin mixture of blood and rainwater, and he left a trail of pinkish spatter as he climbed up the stairs. He changed into dry clothes and crawled into bed. He turned on the news.

Outbreak, panic, blah, blah, blah.

He slept.

Outside, the rain roared.

ATTENTION
BY ORDER OF THE U.S. DEPARTMENT OF
HOMELAND SECURITY

1. All healthy individuals are ORDERED to immediately report to Busch Stadium, West Entrance, St. Louis, Missouri, United States of America for examination by the Centers for Disease Control and Prevention.

2. You will be provided food, clean water, and shelter, and you will be generously compensated.

3. You will provide a blood sample for use in the development of a vaccine for the Medusa virus.

4. Failure to comply with this directive shall constitute a federal crime pursuant to Title 18 of the United States Code.

Signed,

Thomas Roberts, Acting Secretary of Homeland Security

Nathan Crosby, President of the United States of America

GOD BLESS AMERICA

10

Captain Sarah Wells wanted a cigarette, but the respirator covering her face, already busy giving her a bad case of claustrophobia, had made that impossible. She would have been happy with just about any distraction, a piece of gum, a goddamn Tootsie Pop would do at this point, anything that would take her mind off her current reality, walking a turn in the week-old Bronx Quarantine on August 15. She double-checked the thick canvas strap of the M4 rifle around her neck, which she hated using because of the way it chafed her skin, and set her hands on the small of her back, trying to break up some of the tightness that had drawn her muscles taut. It felt like someone had been slowly using a handcrank on her back.

Dawn was breaking in the east, the night slowly

morphing into a dull grayness. A crescent moon hung
low in the lightening sky like a smirk. They were in a
mixed commercial/residential district near the Harlem
River, fertile ground for the symbiotic relationship
between the residents of the brownstones and the
shopkeepers whose bodegas dotted the strip. As it had
been for hours, it was drizzling, the worst kind of rain,
the kind that did nothing to cool you off. Sarah kept
hoping the shower would just metastasize into a downpour, perhaps break the padlock of humidity holding
the city in its clutches, but the drip-drip-drip just kept
on, maddeningly, infuriatingly so, against her stan-
dard-issue helmet. There must have been a hole in her
rain poncho, because she could feel rainwater damp-
ening her fatigues, and the cold squishiness of the
fabric against her hip. The air stank of smoke and
diesel, the smells intensified by the humidity and
wrapping around her in a sweaty fog. She was tired, so
tired. She'd grabbed a few hours of sleep after dinner,
but it had been thin, right at the edge of waking.

Her platoon was stationed on the northeast side of
the Third Avenue Bridge in the Bronx, which separated this borough from northern Manhattan. They'd
blocked each of the two spurs that ran north into the
neighborhood. The canopy had been removed from
her truck, to make room for the Browning .50-caliber
machine gun mounted in the truck's bed. The gun was
a monstrous, serpent-like thing that Sarah could not

keep her eyes off, as if it might come to life and swallow her whole. It was one thing to see it overseas, but she could not imagine having to call that thing into service in the Bronx. Yet there it was, its ammunition belts draped over it like a pageant sash. The platoons had set up sawhorses with electronic displays to fill in the gaps, their orange lights blinking disinterestedly. A series of messages cycled through the digital display, leaving no doubt about the Army's purpose here.

QUARANTINE
NO ACCESS
DEADLY FORCE AUTHORIZED

There had been twenty of them on this detail at the beginning, at the top of the southwest spur. They were down to ten now. Eight had fallen ill with Medusa in the first two days and rotated out, and two more had simply bugged out and gone AWOL. Nearly all of the others were now complaining of symptoms, but the battalion commander had told her not to expect any additional relief for ill soldiers. They were just going to have to man up with ibuprofen and NyQuil. Her two other platoons, stationed farther north along the Harlem River, were reporting similar rates of attrition, but the quarantines were holding. Forget the fact that they were holding because almost everyone inside the quarantine zones was dead. Incidental, and not to cloud the success of the objective.

Sarah herself still felt fine physically, experiencing none of the symptoms the others had described. Two were laid up in the covered truck, too sick to man their posts, and honestly, Sarah didn't know what to do for them. It was all they could do to keep the perimeter secure; things inside the quarantine zone were deteriorating by the day, pressure building up like a failing nuclear reactor. The civilians were sick, angry, and spoiling for a fight. The Bronx hospitals were overwhelmed, turning away patients now, and they'd been left to hear the pleading and the begging from the ones still feeling well enough to be up and around.

That she herself was standing here at all was probably prima facie evidence of sheer insanity, but it wasn't like she'd had any choice in the matter. She didn't want to be here, she didn't want to be anywhere in New York, thank you very much. She'd be lying if she said she hadn't thought about running. She could've run, she supposed, like Lowell and Hewitt had, it was something she was sure they'd all considered, but she never would. She would think about her brother, who had died in Afghanistan, and her dad, a retired mailman who never shut up about how proud he was of her, and she couldn't stand to think she had let them down. And she never forgot that she was a female combat soldier, a *black* female combat soldier, one of the few female officers at Fort Dix.

Her dad, a widower, lived in Raleigh. She wondered how he was, what the story was down there. Fresh, reliable news had become scarce in the last twenty-four hours, nothing but platitudes from the battalion commander that the situation was under control. But if that were true, why were they hearing slices of insanity from the locals, the ones inside the quarantine zone who said the outbreak was getting worse, that the quarantines were collapsing, that no one really had any plan to bring this under control? And some of the estimated casualty figures, if they were to be believed, had made Sarah's legs buckle. Ten million dead. Fifty million dead. Tens of millions infected. No cure.

Rolling into the Bronx had been the most bizarre experience of her life. They had come across the Third Avenue Bridge over the Harlem River, one of many Army units sealing off the bridges into and out of the Bronx. She'd felt on edge during the entire rollout, believing the slightest misstep would cut her, and the unease had grown with each passing hour. Her tours in Afghanistan and Iraq, those had been bad enough, but those were the right kind of scary, the kind she'd expected when she'd joined ROTC her freshman year at SUNY-Albany.

From the passenger seat of the Army truck, she had

looked over her shoulder into the cargo area, into the respirator-covered faces of her subordinates. Their average age was about twenty, meaning that these men, boys really, were only about one Olympics removed from sprouting their first pubes. Barely boys. Babies. Many of them had still been in diapers when the Twin Towers came down.

"Captain Wells."

The voice startled her. It seemed like hours had passed since anyone had said anything. The platoons had been pacing nonstop, carving grooves into the asphalt, nervously looking at one another as the minutes ticked by. She looked up and saw Private Qureshi jogging toward her, his arm pointed north, into the quarantine zone. He was one of the youngest in the platoon, rail thin, a sweet kid, a good soldier. He was sweating and his cheeks were flushed, but she tried to ignore that.

"Something's going on," he said. "Inside the Q zone."

"What is it?"

"Not sure," he said. "This seems organized." He coughed twice, and Sarah's heart broke. She didn't understand how this could be happening, how this thing was spreading the way it was. They were wearing the masks. The fucking masks!

"You feeling OK?"

"Fine," he said. "Fine."

She could see the panic in his eyes; he finally had the answer to the question she'd asked herself a million times – when was she going to start coughing and roasting with fever, when would the blood start pouring from her nose and ears? If anything, she'd fully expected to be one of the first to get sick, but here she was, more than a week since this thing had blown up, and she still felt fine.

The universe, she did have a sense of humor, didn't she?

She followed Qureshi around the truck, toward the intersection of Lincoln Avenue and Bruckner Boulevard, where they'd established the perimeter. As she came around the front grill of the truck, she saw a crowd forming in a parking lot to the east, swaying back and forth, buzzing with chatter. Two of her soldiers were walking toward the group, their rifles up, trying to wave them off. Within seconds, people were yelling at the troops, getting up in their covered faces, almost as if they'd been waiting for them.

An angry undercurrent rippled through the crowd, the inverse of a happy summer block party. There were hundreds of people, of all colors and ethnicities, milling about. Flushed faces, shirts dark with sweat, eyes hollow and sunken. The sidewalks were narrow and jammed, a stinking, nervous mass of humanity rippling in the virgin light of the morning. She could hear people sniffling, sneezing, coughing, deep, ripping coughs exploding like hidden land mines.

Sarah jumped back in her truck and activated the built-in megaphone.

"Return to your homes," Sarah called out, her amplified voice laced with static and sounding far away, like it was too far away to do any good. "You are interfering with a military quarantine."

This only antagonized the crowd, and the buzz continued to amplify. Replies mingled together to form a loud symphony of anger and frustration. Behind her, she could hear the troops yelling and cussing, the sounds of magazines being locked and loaded.

The soldiers fanned out around the truck, forming a defensive perimeter, their rifles up and pointed at their fellow citizens. Out of the corner of her eye, Sarah saw another throng approaching from the east, via a side street, hidden just so by the bodega on the corner. She didn't like this. It appeared coordinated, as if the locals had decided they'd had just about enough of their party guests and had stayed up all night coming up with a plan to rid themselves of their company. She activated her shoulder mike.

"Echo Three to Echo Base," Sarah said. "We need backup. A large crowd of civilians, possibly turning hostile."

As she waited for a reply, an organized mass of young men, white, black, Asian, Latino, formed on the southwest corner, blocking their continued progress north and drawing the attention of her platoon. Two of her soldiers, the two oldest in the platoon, stepped forward.

"Negative, Echo Three. Good luck," said Lt. Col. Craig Curwood, the commanding officer in the Bronx.

Jesus.

If Echo Base had bigger priorities than a dozen American soldiers trapped by an angry and armed mob, it was going to be a very, very long day.

A gunshot broke her out of her trance, and that was when Captain Sarah Wells knew things had changed forever and irrevocably so. Without thinking, she dropped prone, the way she had in Kandahar Province and Iraq, in tours and days gone by, the ground knocking the wind out of her. Two feet in front of her, Private First Class Wally Griffin failed to move fast enough. His big body, six-four, 220 pounds of unfulfilled dreams of life as a Division I quarterback at Alabama or Tennessee, some good SEC school, seized up for a moment, just a flash of a second, and then he fell to the ground like he'd dropped through a trap door.

"No, no, no!" Sarah groaned.

From her stomach, Sarah aimed her weapon high and squeezed off two shots. This was by instinct, years of training imprinted on her, almost like a brand. Executed like a computer program, and that was for the best because she had just fired her weapon on U.S. soil, on American citizens, and, the worst part of it was that she was defending herself and her troops. Before the thought could overwhelm her, flood her engine, she slid up to Griffin's side and found him still. There was a small dime-sized hole just over his left eye, and an exit wound the size of a silver dollar at the base of his skull. Blood was pooling underneath him, the dark red liquid staining the asphalt.

As Sarah tended to her dying charge, a burst of small-arms fire erupted near her – from whom, she couldn't tell, and in the end, did it even matter? Howls of agony and terror followed as the 5.56x45mm NATO rounds in her platoon's M4s found targets, thick, heavy thumps as the big rounds slammed into dense flesh, cutting through muscle and bone like teeth into a rare steak. Many scattered at the exchange of gunfire, but some remained, and Sarah was sickened to see the ones that stuck around were armed, intent on continuing this insanity. One of her soldiers, maybe Private Woods, was caught in a no-man's-land, and two unseen gunmen opened up on him, raking his legs with a hail of large-caliber bullets. There was no precision to the attack, just some lunatics unloading their semi-automatic pistols. Woods dropped to the ground, writhing in pain. Two other soldiers lay down fire as they tried to recover their fallen brother.

Back to her shoulder mike. Certainly, Echo Base would want to know about American soldiers engaged in a firefight with American citizens in the fucking

Bronx on a Saturday morning, right? They hadn't seem concerned with any of the other status updates she'd called in, but this would be different, she told herself. If not, well, Echo Base could go fuck itself.

"Echo Base, Echo Three is fully engaged," she said, tipping her head toward her shoulder mike, shouting over another staccato M4 burst. "Requesting helicopter support, goddammit!"

This time, Echo Base didn't make her wait long, barely an instant.

"Request denied," came the reply, sounding far away and emotionless. "Echo Three, you are ordered to maintain the quarantine by any means necessary. Acknowledge."

Sarah felt every muscle in her body tighten up like she'd been hit with an electrical current. Around her, the small arms fire was intensifying, almost like a Fourth of July fireworks show reaching its final crescendo. Most of the gunfire was of the M4 variety, the sound as familiar to her as her own voice, but there were still others woven into the fabric of the gunbattle, .38 specials and SIG Sauers from dusty shoeboxes on closet shelves, possibly a MAC-10 in there. Street guns, no match for the military hardware Echo Three was packing.

Any means necessary.

Jesus. So this was for real. Really real. Her mind went blank and she let herself be the soldier she'd trained for more than a decade to become. Not for the first time in her life, she was thankful for her Army training. She was trained to follow orders, and it let her detach from the current reality. Many times, it was the job that had drawn her through the darkest times in her life. She had to believe this terrible order she'd been given, one that would surely haunt her for the rest of her days, however many of them remained, was being issued for the greater good. That thoughtful, careful, deliberate men had examined the situation here and the situation elsewhere and determined that this was the only way.

"Acknowledge, Echo Three."

"By any means necessary," Wells repeated. "Copy that."

"God bless you, Echo Three," came the reply, the voice softer this time, followed by a quick burst of static. Then silence.

This made Sarah's blood run cold, and a hard shiver rippled through her body. Using the helmet-com, she switched the channel over to the platoon's dedicated frequency.

"Echo Three, fall back!" she barked.

After clicking off her communicator, she did a quick recon of their situation. Multiple casualties, multiple itchy trigger fingers and their scared shitless captain. Immediately to her left, four soldiers – Preston Beaumont, Johnny Weekes, Clint Vranian and Faisal

Qureshi. Quite a quartet, she thought. All barely out of basic training. The others were scattered around the perimeter of the truck. Just ahead was a side street, an alley more than anything, which cut behind a bodega; she took note of it as a possible escape route in case they needed to get out quickly. That's what it had come to. Planning a possible bugout.

"Our orders are to maintain the quarantine by any means necessary," she said after they had congregated behind the truck.

"Fuck that!" came the deep, bellowing voice of PFC Vinnie Matthews. He'd been sick since midnight. "What the fuck is the point of all this? We're all fucking dead anyway! I fucking quit."

Without thinking about it, Sarah drove the butt of her rifle into Matthews' midsection; when he doubled over, grunting, coughing up blood, she brought up her right knee squarely into his chin. She laid him down gently on the ground and knelt down close to him, his panic-stricken face just inches from her own.

"Don't ever question my orders again," she said softly.

Matthews nodded, his eyes shiny with tears. She eyed him for a moment longer, debating whether she should try and give him a comforting word. She decided against it. They were all in the same sinking boat.

"Anyone else want to fucking quit?" she asked,

surveying the faces of her terrified troops.

"We have a fucking job to do," she said when no one replied. "I don't know what the fuck is going on, or how long we're going to be here, but we have to believe our orders are part of some bigger plan to get us out of this shit. Are we clear?"

A gaggle of "Ma'ams" and "Yes ma'ams" followed. She didn't know if they believed what she was saying; she wasn't sure she believed it. But if she didn't *act* like she believed it, she'd lose whatever thread of control she maintained over her platoon.

"All right, let's get back to work."

In the distance, she heard shouts, some English, some Spanish, still others in languages she didn't recognize. Gunshots peppered the air, the smell of smoke and metal intensifying. She peered around the front edge of the truck, back toward the quarantine zone and saw another crowd forming, this one louder and angrier than the first. Pockets of people swarmed the area, people hiding behind parked vehicles, in alleys, behind the buildings. She saw many were armed this time, the mob evolving like a strain of deadly bacteria. Movement along the tops of the buildings near the perimeter caught her eye, and she realized with horror these people were getting ready to launch some kind of offensive against her unit.

"Weekes!" she barked into her communicator. "Looks like we've got movement on the rooftops."

As if on cue, a hail of gunfire rained down on them from above. Sarah and Weekes turned and directed their fire on the rooftop snipers. She fired one burst, and then another, and then another, her M4 growing hot in her hands. Weekes edged around the far side of the truck and came up firing, but the shooter retreated from the edge. Then she turned her attention toward the clusters, crying as she cut down citizen after citizen.

A loud, revving groan caught her attention, and she swung her gaze toward the source of the noise. A large vehicle was accelerating toward the roadblock, coming from the north, possibly a moving van or delivery truck. As it breached the last roadblock-free intersection, hell erupted around Sarah. The street exploded with heavy gunfire. She rotated back around the front of the truck and opened up with her M4, tears streaming down her cheeks, partially from fear, but mostly from sadness, terrible, crushing sadness that her life was probably going to end here, in New York City, everything fucked six ways to Sunday.

"I'll man the gun!" she shouted. Her heavy footsteps twanged against the metal bed of the truck, and within seconds, the air was filled with the terrifying whisper of the .50-caliber gun as its rounds found purchase in the front grill of the truck. The machine gun edged upwards slightly, just a hair, and within a second, a splatter of red splashed against the windshield. But it was too late. The truck's trajectory shifted slightly, as it continued without human control, but it didn't decelerate at all.

"Fall back!" she screamed.

Realizing there was no chance to divert the truck from its homicidal trajectory, Sarah leapt off the machine gun battery; a second later, the truck's grill crashed into the side of Sarah's armored personnel carrier and it careened up Lincoln Avenue toward the bridge. She hit the ground hard and rolled, her body a rag doll against the rain-slickened asphalt. The truck pitched and yawed as it hit the bridge, scraping up against the left guardrail. It overcorrected, sweeping across the other travel lanes before punching through the guardrail on the north side of the bridge. It plunged sixty feet into the dark waters of the Harlem River, piercing the surface with a terrific slap.

The crowd poured into the gap created by the collision like water from a ruptured main, flowing, flowing, flowing. Sarah scampered out of the way, taking cover under the remains of an old Toyota Celica; she lay prone and watched hundreds, thousands of feet slapping the pavement. She activated her shoulder mike.

"Echo Base, Echo Three."

The open line hissed with static.

"Repeat, Echo Base, Echo Three. Third Avenue Bridge quarantine breached. Repeat. Third Avenue Quarantine breached."

More static. No answer.

Sarah watched them stream through, sick, dying, carrying the virus with them into Harlem. When the flow had tapered to a trickle, she crawled out of her hiding spot, her M4 at the ready. But it wasn't needed. The crowd cascaded across the bridge now, people staggering and stumbling over one another like a haunted funhouse version of a picturesque marathon start.

She had failed.

A buzz drew her attention, and she turned her head south, where she saw two low-flying helicopters following the cut of the river, closing fast. Apaches, loaded for bear. Multiple starbursts winked in the low morning gloom as each chopper unleashed four Hellfire missiles upriver. The rockets screamed north and slammed into the Third Avenue bridge superstructure; it disappeared into a cloud of smoke, debris and body parts. As fifteen hundred men, women and children plunged to their deaths alongside the twisted, burning wreckage of the bridge, the screams were so loud, so piercing it made Sarah's head throb.

When it was over, the Apaches dipped their noses low, as if sighing, and continued upriver. A strange silence enveloped everything around her, and Sarah stood there watching the burning rubble and bodies floating in the Harlem River.

INTERLUDE

FROM SELECTED TWITTER ACCOUNTS

Hashtags #Medusa #plague #flu

August 15

9:16 a.m. to 9:17 a.m. Eastern Daylight Time

@NewYorkCity: Quarantines will remain in effect until further notice #Medusa

@LynnSwanson: The hospitals are full here in Topeka. Please spread the word #Medusa #flu

@Andre2K: Bodies stacked up on outskirts of town. Long ditch being dug. #Bozeman #Medusa #cobra

@JavierWriter: I just saw a policeman shoot and kill two looters! #cleveland #medusa #plague

@CarlosDiaz: Todo el mundo en mi edificio está muerto! Tengo una fiebre. #medusa #ayudar

@USHomelandSecurity: A #Medusa vaccine is nearly ready for widespread distribution

@NBCNews: RT @USHomelandSecurity: A

#Medusa vaccine is nearly ready for widespread distribution

@TadMcGuire: Sounds of heavy gunfire all night long. So scared. #trustinjesus #medusa

@ErinCollins: here's a pic of the fire at Murfreesboro water tower. No firetrucks!!! #medusa #tennessee

@DesMoinesEmergencyOps: Please mark an X on your front door for body removal #medusa

@VanceBaker22: It is time to make your peace with YOUR LORD! The TIME OF THE RAPTURE IS AT HAND! #medusa

@WorldNews: #Medusa outbreaks reported in London, New Delhi, Tokyo. Mortality exceeding 90 percent in some areas. North Korea reporting no infections.

@PastorJohn: #Medusa is God's judgment on our wicked world! The fag marriages and the homos are to blame!

11

Whenthe end came for his seven-year-old Heather, the last surviving member of his family, Freddie Briggs was holding her hand, sitting on a cold metal chair next to her bed. As she slipped away, he made no attempt to hale a nurse or flag down a doctor or otherwise ignite the engine of modern medicine. Instead, he squeezed her hand and whispered in her ear, knowing from the countless explosions of grief that had rocked the intensive care unit throughout the day that no one was going to do anything, that no one *could* do anything. Everyone in the hospital was stumbling drunk through a surrealistic minefield, the landscape getting smokier with panic and misery with each passing hour.

In her last terrible moments, Heather seized briefly and then her body simply shut down. It was the

quickest and least traumatic of the deaths of the three
people Freddie loved more than anything in the world.
She didn't seem to be in any pain, but wasn't that what
they all said? How the hell did anyone know that
anyway? She was lying perfectly still, her eyes closed,
as they had been for the last six hours. Freddie folded
her hands over her heart, brushed her hair, which had
been matted down around her face with sweat, out of
her eyes, and then sat back in his metal folding chair.

He became very aware of an itch on his neck and
scratched it. The relief was huge, the sound of the
fingernail scraping the dry patch of skin more soothing
than seemed normal. He looked at his watch; it was
six-fifteen. A perfectly ordinary time of day, with its
own rituals and routines. Dinnertime. The early
SportsCenter. Happy hour.

Freddie looked around the room that had become
the Briggs family crypt and wondered what the hell
good this private hospital room had done for his Susan
and Caroline and Heather. Not a goddamn thing. As he
thought about the last few days, he felt tears sliding
down his cheek, and he wiped them away with the
back of his hand.

By the time the ambulance had pulled away from
the Briggs house, Susan and Caroline were both symptomatic. Susan had been the sicker of the two, wors-
ening by the minute. Her chest was rising and falling
quickly as her body struggled to draw in oxygen. Pale

on her healthiest days, Susan's skin had taken on an ashy tone and was stretched taut against her already thin frame, as though it had shrunk and no longer fit. One of the paramedics, the teacher, kept attaching and reattaching a blood-pressure cuff, seemingly unhappy with the results he was getting. As the ambulance rounded a corner, he felt Susan's body heave, and she began coughing, an interminable spasm that didn't subside until they'd made it to the hospital.

Freddie was thrilled they'd been assigned the last available room, and he tried not to think about the fact they'd been afforded that luxury because for the first time in his life, Freddie had used the "Don't you know who I am?" card. As it turned out, the staffer in charge of room assignment had known who he was; she and her husband were huge Falcons fans, hopeful they could afford to get season tickets this year, but it would probably be next year. She had prattled on and on about football while working to check them in, apparently oblivious to the fact that things were going straight to hell, and Briggs had indulged her only because he had hoped it meant they'd get seen faster.

They probably had gotten seen faster, but in the end it hadn't mattered. Susan died within an hour of checking into the room, despite an exhausted-looking doctor doing his best to keep her airway open. Freddie had begged him to tell him what was going on, how could so many have gotten so sick so fast, what the plan was to treat his family. The man hadn't replied, and after he'd given up his resuscitation efforts, he simply said he was sorry and disappeared from the room. Caroline died two days after they checked in; Heather, the littlest one, fought the hardest, her body standing its ground for days, much longer than virtually anyone else in the unit, but eventually, she too, began to lose her battle.

As Heather deteriorated, Freddie began to realize the din, the frantic shouts of physicians' orders and medications and codes, was nothing more than busy work, a desperate attempt to make it look like there was still order and structure in the hospital, because admitting that there was no order or structure would be like a boxer quitting on his stool in between rounds, throwing the blood- and snot-soaked towel into the middle of the ring. Brief sorties out of the room to get ice or juice or towels or just to see what the hell was going on had told him all he needed to know. So he just sat there with his beloved daughter, feeling oddly empty inside, as if the parts that had made Freddie Briggs Freddie Briggs had been scooped out with a shovel, and he was just the shell left behind.

Freddie sat back down in his chair and let out a long sigh. The machines in the room, a heart monitor and an IV cart, were silent. He hadn't seen a nurse or doctor in about ten hours, not since Caroline had died in his arms earlier that morning, crying and coughing blood and writhing until she'd simply gone limp, a puppet with its strings cut. The doctor, ill himself with Medusa, had stood there, hugging them both, crying and apologizing. After it was over, the doctor had fled the room like it was on fire, shouting garbled nonsense. No one had made a pronouncement of death, no one had signed a death certificate, and no one had come to remove the body.

Her small body was wrapped with a bedsheet, tucked in the corner of their room because Freddie Briggs hadn't had the first fucking clue what, precisely, he was supposed to do with the dead body of one daughter while watching the life drain out of the other.

The dead had been cast wherever there was open space, in some places two on a gurney. And they were the lucky ones. Many had been lined up on the bright, cold tile floors, under sheets and blankets, and they had simply died there, having never received a single second of treatment. The other rooms had been crammed full of patients, haphazardly triaged by the stage of infection. Adherence to universal precautions had long been abandoned; the intensive care unit was covered in blood and all manner of bodily fluids, but no one had bothered to clean it up.

He watched a fly (and there seemed to be a lot of flies buzzing around this evening) land on his daughter's nose, and that was when it finally hit him. His sweet, gentle, serious Heather was gone, like her sister and their mother, leaving him all alone in a world disintegrating around him. Heather had loved her hamster and their two family cats, and since she'd been old enough to understand the concept of veterinary medicine, that's what she'd wanted to do with her life. Never once had she wavered, never once had she talked about becoming a princess or a nurse or a professional soccer player. She bought books about animals by the armful and loved going to the zoo, even though she'd been torn on the whole concept of zoos and whether it was thoughtful conservation or just plain cruel to the animals, and just like that she was dead.

His family was dead.

"My wife is dead," he said to the empty room. "My daughters are dead."

The room remained silent.

He said it again.

"My family is dead."

He turned on the television with the remote control.

Why had he done that?

He didn't know.

The television was tuned to the NBC affiliate, but it was drawing the MSNBC feed for some reason. Onscreen, the words ON THE PHONE: *Lenox Bowman, Byron, MN*, were superimposed over a graphic of a rotary telephone.

"...we're just praying real hard, Megan," a voice was saying, but Freddie tuned the voice out because he didn't want to hear what Lenox Bowman from Byron, Minnesota had to say about anything, thank you very much.

At the top of the screen were the words **NATION IN CRISIS**. At the bottom was the ubiquitous crawl, the ticker relaying undoubtedly important information about wearing facemasks or eating chicken soup and staying in bed or whatever. And that wasn't all. Somehow, the genius producer had managed to slap the number for the Centers for Disease Control on there as well, and it all swirled together in a miasma of nonsense until he changed the channel.

Modern Family was on.

Much better than Lenox Bowman from Byron, Minnesota!

He watched two episodes. One of them he'd seen before, but the second was new to him. Weird that he'd missed an episode of *Modern Family*! Susan used to DVR it for him, and they'd watch it together before bed. Susan.

He changed the channel again. A nature show talking about the blue-footed booby, and this seemed soothing in its own way, so he left it on. Then he sat back down in his metal chair because he really didn't know what he was supposed to do now. He sat there for another ten minutes. Then he went over to the door and cracked it open, just a sliver, not wanting to draw any attention to himself. If he turned his head just right, he could make out the nurses' station at the center of the floor. Everything was still chaotic, still madness, a giant sewage-like wave of horror washing across the cold tile floors, engulfing all in its path. A tall, skinny man, pacing back and forth in front of the nurses' station, arguing with two nurses inexplicably still on duty. Few were still working, and Freddie didn't know if that was because they'd fled the hospital or if they were now patients themselves. He wondered where his agent Richie was.

The man was shirtless, his chest speckled with blood and Lord knew what else. Freddie heard moaning in other rooms, and of course, the wet, ripping sound of that horrible cough that had become the background music to the disintegration of the hospital. On the far side of the nurses' station, a middle-aged man wearing a perfectly nice Hawaiian shirt was arguing with a doctor about something or the other. He became increasingly animated, and then Freddie watched, stunned, as Hawaiian-Shirt Man plunged a white plastic knife into the doctor's throat.

As blood began spurting from doctor's wounded neck, Freddie slammed the door shut and slid down on his bottom. There just wasn't enough room in his brain to deal with such insanity. He held his huge hands over his ears as the volume ramped up. A shout, then another, and then a gunshot. Freddie heard heavy footsteps race past his door, and that was when he started to wonder why he hadn't come down with it, why he hadn't started coughing up blood and burning with the terrible fever that had taken everything he had ever known and loved. Until now, he hadn't had time to think about it, but now that he did, he felt fine, just fine, and he believed it had been because he had to be there for Susan and Caroline and Heather as they grew sicker and sicker, as they died, and he sure as hell wasn't going to let them die alone.

But now they were gone, and he didn't care about feeling fine. He didn't care about feeling anything because feeling meant thinking about them and the fact that they were dead and gone. How could they be dead? Caroline was supposed to start the seventh grade in two weeks, Heather, the third grade. Susan was a kindergarten teacher and she was about to start getting her classroom ready, one of the things she enjoyed the most about a new school year. He found himself thinking about the glitter and glue sticks and pencil boxes and Back to School Night, which would make Susan so nervous she barely slept the night before, and the classroom's guinea pig, which was now three years old. Or was it four?

Then the most ridiculous thought zoomed through Freddie's head as he sat there on the cold tile floor, in the company of his dead family.

Who was going to feed the guinea pig?

The guinea pig. The guinea pig. He kept thinking about the guinea pig, skittering around its cage in their family room, where Susan kept him during summer vacation. Freddie hadn't spent more than thirty seconds of his life thinking about the goddamn guinea pig, and now it was all he could think about. Chewie the guinea pig, with his pink-rimmed eyes and the light brown spot on his back.

Who was going to feed the guinea pig?

He was crying again, big silent tears streaming down his face. The room seemed very small, as if the walls were closing in around him. He became aware of the smell, the sourness of his own body odor, the rich, gassy smell of decay in the room, and he saw the blood and vomit and the other byproducts of death to which he'd somehow remained oblivious for the past few days. But now it was all coming home, the true reality of what had happened, and he needed to get out of this room right now, right away. Part of him, the responsible family man part of him, told himself to stay right where he was because his place was by his family's side, but its voice was growing weaker and fainter, and he needed to get out of this hospital right now.

He kissed his three girls on their foreheads, and then gently set Susan and Heather's bodies next to Caroline's. He wasn't going to stay here in this house of death, and, he decided, neither was the rest of the

Briggs clan. After covering their bodies with a sheet and locking the bedrails, he pushed the bed out of the room, nearly blinded by the tears, almost hoping someone would try and stop him.

No one did, no one even gave him a second look as he wheeled the bed down to the elevators at the far end of the hallway, moving slowly so as not to jostle his precious cargo. The elevator vestibule was dark, empty but for a dead woman and the now-lifeless body of Hawaiian Shirt Man. The floor under his body was shiny with blood.

Freddie wasn't sure if the elevators were working, but the call button lit up like a solitary Christmas light when he pressed it. He considered his next move as the elevator hummed its way to the fourth floor. Home was his final destination; he was going to get his girls home where they belonged, and if that meant he was going to bury them in their backyard, then so be it. He'd be damned if he was going to let them rot here in this hellhole, in this dead place. If he had to carry them the four miles, then that's what he would do.

The familiar *bing* broke him out of his trance, and he prepared to roll the bed into the elevator. As it opened, he changed his mind. Three plague victims were lying on the floor of the elevator, dead or very close to it. One appeared to be a doctor, his white lab coat streaked with blood. He was on his back, his eyes fixed on the ceiling, and he was moaning softly. He either did not notice Freddie's presence or simply paid it no mind. And the smell was what Freddie really noticed, an overpowering stench of raw death that sent Freddie's stomach into revolt. One whiff, and he was doubled over, dry heaving because, since he hadn't eaten in more than a day, there was nothing to bring up. As Freddie struggled to catch his breath, the heaves stealing his ability to breathe, the dying doctor rolled over on his side and flung his arm out across the threshold of the elevator. When the door tried to slide home, it met the doctor's arm and then bounced back open again.

The hell with this, Freddie thought, as his stomach began to settle down. He said a little prayer for his family, asked God for strength for what he was about to do, and then slung Susan's body over his right shoulder, the girls' bodies over his left. The stairwell was just beyond the elevators, and he carried them down the four flights like sacks of flour, taking special care not to bang their bodies against the rails or the walls. At each landing, he found more of the sick and the dead, bodies sprawled everywhere, and he stepped carefully so as not to trip. He was a little winded by the time he got to the first floor, but his legs were strong. He was thankful for the six months he'd spent running and weightlifting. It hadn't been to make it back to the NFL, he now understood; it had been so he could be strong enough to take his family home one final time.

More chaos greeted him on the first floor of the hospital as he burst out of the stairwell, possibly even more than he'd left behind on the fourth floor. Bodies lined the corridor, stacked one on top of the other like firewood, double-wide in some places, leaving barely enough room for two people to pass each other in the hallway. Here and there, he'd see someone stumbling around, the look of someone who was lost, eyes open but far away. It was warm down here, the air stale and thick with an oppressive stench Freddie couldn't identify, that he didn't particularly want to identify. He spotted one of his neighbors, a pleasant stay-at-home mom named Meg Tinsley, sitting on the floor, weeping. She didn't appear to have seen him, and so he kept on walking, unsure of what the hell he would even say to her.

No one paid him any mind as he staggered through the white corridors, through the emergency department, past the curtained areas and the gurneys. Any semblance of order in the hospital had crumbled like a cookie in a child's hand. The unit was drenched with moans and howls, a terrible soundtrack to this constantly evolving and endless horror show. The main entrance was blocked by an ambulance that had crashed through the doors.

He kept moving, past the ER and into another series of corridors. Panic chewed at his insides like a rat as each of the corridors began to look more and more alike. At a large intersection, where he saw signs directing visitors to cardiology and radiology and physical therapy and other perfectly ordinary hospital destinations, he saw two dead doctors sitting on the floor, backs to the wall; their hands were laced together, dried blood caked on their faces and lab coats. One of the doctors even had a chart set on her lap, God bless her little heart. As he gazed down on these two, he wondered if he would have the courage to stay and treat the sick if he'd found themselves in their shoes. He began to cry because he wouldn't have stayed if he were one of these doctors. He would have fled, he knew it as deeply and as surely as he'd ever known anything in his life.

As he turned left at a bank of elevators, he finally spotted the reassuring red glow of an Exit sign, and his heart soared. It was bad in here, much worse than he'd ever imagined, and he wanted to get out of here more than he'd ever wanted anything in his life. Part of him couldn't believe how widespread this thing was, but he pushed those thoughts out of his head as he continued his funereal procession. There would be time for that later; right now, his focus was on getting his family home. And besides, what difference did it make how far the disease had spread? His own universe had imploded, taking with it all the galaxies and stars of his soul.

He turned a corner and saw the main foyer ahead

of him, but it looked nothing like the one he'd seen when they'd checked into three days ago. It was a dead place, crowded with the bodies of plague victims who had died waiting to be seen. The Exit sign glowed ominously, a deep warning shade of red. A makeshift wall of sandbags bisected the foyer, and a pair of unmanned machine gun batteries had been mounted there, the turrets pointed in opposite directions. Freddie puzzled over the scene for a moment, trying to ascertain what had happened here, but his head began to swim with confusion. Nothing he'd seen in the last seventy-two hours had made a lick of sense.

The foyer was silent but for the heavy breathing of a National Guardsman curled up in the corner, where the sandbags met the glass wall. At first, Freddie couldn't tell if the man was conscious; then the soldier looked up at him, his M4 rifle pointed squarely at Freddie's chest. He was a young guy, a thin wisp of mustache coloring his upper lip. His name patch identified him as Barousse.

"Not supposed to leave the hospital," Barousse eked out.

"Please leave me alone," Freddie said.

"Quarantine," he said. "The quarantine broke."

"What the fuck is going on out there?" Freddie asked. "What happened?"

"No one-" A spasm of coughing interrupted, and thin, ropy splatters of blood sprayed the soldier's pant

legs. Private Barousse wiped his mouth with the back
of his gloved hand and examined the residue of his
spittle.

"What a Charlie Foxtrot this turned out to be,"
Barousse said.

"A what?"

"Cluster fuck."

"What happened?" Freddie asked again.

"Not really sure," Barousse said. "Things just
fucked up."

He sighed deeply.

"Hey man, do you have a cigarette? I'm sleepy."

He leaned his head back against the glass and
closed his eyes. Freddie paused for a moment, sorry he
didn't have a cigarette, hoping the soldier didn't intend
to enforce the quarantine that no longer existed, and
then swung his legs over the sandbag barrier, one at a
time. The hospital's main doors slid open, and Freddie
stepped out into the bright August afternoon, the sun
harsh and merciless. His eyes adjusted to the glare, but
slowly, as if they didn't believe what they were seeing,
hesitant to report the images back to Freddie's brain.

Two Georgia National Guard trucks were parked in
the semi-circular drive at the main entrance; one of
them was barely recognizable, its front end a smol-
dering husk, thin wisps of smoke still drifting from the
engine block. The street fronting the hospital was
barricaded at both ends by police cruisers, but Freddie

couldn't tell if anyone was manning the roadblocks. On the south side of the street was the hospital's main parking lot, where a ring of police cars had set up shop around the perimeter. The parking lot itself was not particularly crowded with cars, as only about half the spots were occupied. The driving lanes, however, were lined with rows of cylindrically shaped objects of varying sizes, shrouded in white. Freddie stared at it for a moment and then froze, his eyes locked on the rows, knowing what he was seeing, but not wanting to accept it. He forced himself to break eye contact and headed north along the street, the image of the shrouds strong and bright in his memory, like marquees on Broadway.

The parking lot had become a mass grave.

INTERLUDE

FROM NATIONAL SECURITY AGENCY LISTENING POST
0451029

August 16

    0345 Greenwich Mean Time

    Bekaa Valley, Lebanon

    Unsub: Unknown Subject

    AAN: Ahmad Abu-Nidal, Second-in-Command of Dawn of God

    Translated from Arabic

TRANSMISSION BEGINS

Unsub: What the hell is going on?

AAN: I do not know. An evil eye is watching down on us. [COUGHING]

Unsub: No way this happened naturally.

AAN: Regardless of how it is happening, it is happening. [WHEEZING, COUGHING]

Unsub: They are going to blame us. You know that, yes?

AAN: Yes, but I do not think it matters.

Unsub: How could it not matter? They will scorch the earth looking for us. Do you know how many have died in America alone?

AAN: Do you know where I am right now? [COUGHING]

Unsub: Don't you dare!

AAN: I am just north of Ain Hirshey. Have you heard of it?

Unsub: No. My God, they'll be on you in a day.

AAN: It's a little village in the mountains. Barely a village, really.

Unsub: And I care about this why?

AAN: Because every single person in this town is dead. The last village, dead. The village before that one. Dead.

Unsub: How does that impact us?

AAN: You fool. This sickness is everywhere. There won't be anyone left to look for us. I've spoken to our comrades in China and Russia and South America, and there it is the same.

Unsub: God is great! The pigs will die.

AAN: [LAUGHTER, FOLLOWED BY COUGHING]

Unsub: What is so funny?

AAN: God might be great, but he is also pissed.

Unsub: God be with you.

AAN: Go to hell.

TRANSMISSION ENDS

INTERLUDE

FROM THE SUICIDE NOTE OF WILLIAM BRADY

Knoxville, TN

Undated

I'm sorry. I'm so sorry. I thought this would be so much different. I used to think an apocalypse would be cool. I liked zombie movies and *The Stand* and those kinds of books and movies and I thought it would be cool to be a survivor. And here I am. I'm a survivor and I didn't get sick and I watched my mom and my four sisters die in the last five days and it was the worst fucking thing you could imagine. And I think I might be the last person alive in this shithole city and I'm not exaggerating. I haven't seen a single living person in I don't know how long and we just went and fucked ourselves pretty good didn't we. And it's so QUIET so GODDAMN QUIET I can hear my fucking heart beating! The smell is getting worse because it's been hot and humid this summer and it gets worse after it rains, oh, Jesus, it gets so much worse. I don't know why I'm writing this at all because no one is ever going to read it but I had some things I wanted to say before I did it. I'm so sorry. I'm so afraid & I don't want to be afraid anymore.

If anyone reads this and wants to know, well, let me just tell you, it was so bad, so bad at the end. Everything just went to hell it was like we were animals worse than animals. Sorry, God. We must've really pissed you off.

fuck you.

12

It was August 24.

That was according to Adam's watch, which he found himself looking at with increasing frequency. He wore it all the time now, even when he slept, something he'd never done before. He kept the band tight, to the point that it was chafing his skin, but he wanted to feel it close to his body. It was very important to know what time it was, all the time. He would check it and be a little amused to find that time had continued to tick by as it always had, second by second, minute by minute, Medusa victim by Medusa victim. Time was decidedly unconcerned with the affairs of men. Time didn't care. What, was his watch going to stop ticking because the human race had offed itself?

Then he found himself thinking about the Doomsday Clock, that delicious bit of geopolitical commentary in which a bunch of old farts got together each year and passed judgment on how well the human race had behaved itself, their decision reflected in the minute hand of a giant analog clock set to a few minutes before midnight. The closer humanity got to midnight, the story went, the closer it was to extinction. The last time he'd read about it in *Time* or the *Huffington Post* or what-have-you, the clock had been moved forward three minutes, all the way to 11:57 p.m., thanks to a whole shitload of new problems humanity had created for itself. He wondered what time they'd set the Doomsday Clock to now. Probably two-thirty in the morning. They might even make a little note in their little Diary, if there was such a thing, that not only was it way, way past midnight, but that humanity was stumbling around drunk, vomit on its shirt, looking for a late-night slice of greasy pizza.

Adam was on the couch, his television tuned to ESPN, a bottle of Jack Daniels nestled between his legs. The electricity was still on, and that was one of the few pieces of good news, but he wondered when that bit of luck would run out. Currently, the television cameras were broadcasting from the Bristol, Connecticut studio where they taped SportsCenter – *used* to tape Sports-Center, a little voice squeaked from within – but the place looked abandoned. Someone had left the cameras on and, not surprisingly, no one had been back to turn them off. The camera was still pointed at

the unmanned anchor desk. Off camera, from somewhere deep in the studios, Adam could hear someone
coughing, nearly retching. Adam couldn't bear
to change the channel. He didn't want the person in
the studio to be alone. Maybe if he kept watching, that
poor bastard, dying alone inside the headquarters of
the Worldwide Leader, wouldn't be so alone. It didn't
make a whole lot of sense, but it wasn't like there was
anything else to do anyway.

He took another nip of the amber-colored whisky.
The liquor burned his throat like drain cleaner as it
sloshed its way to his stomach. He considered the last
week of his life, which in many ways had been the final
week of his life, his old life, before he had been birthed
through the blood and viscera of a dying mother into
this new world on the other side of history.

He got up from the couch and wandered over to
the big bay windows looking south onto Floyd Avenue.
It was evening, still light out, but long purple shadows
had just begun to creep across the street and up the
sidewalks, the beginnings of a blanket of twilight on
the city. Night filled him with dread now, as it had
when he was a boy. A random memory from his childhood began playing in his head, like a song from his
iPod set to shuffle. He'd been seven or eight years old,
unable to sleep thanks to the shadows cast by a pair of
saplings outside his bedroom window, shadows that
shimmied in the wind like the bony arms of the

undead, plotting and just waiting for little Adam to fall asleep so they could sneak in his window and cut his throat. Adam crawled down the hall, seeking comfort from his father, who had called him a pussy, smacked him across the side of the head and sent him back to bed.

For the first few days he'd been back in Richmond, he was certain he had to be dreaming. There was simply no way that what was happening was actually happening. Even when he'd reported to the hospital for a marathon three-day shift beginning on the fourteenth, during which he'd made two hundred and fifty-six pronouncements of death, and would have made hundreds more if they'd continued keeping track of them, it had to be a dream. When he told them he was on suspension, and the acting chief of medicine had said he wouldn't have cared if Adam had been a rabid raccoon, it had to be a dream. He watched his patients die, then he watched the nurses and doctors die, and by the time he left on the afternoon of the seventeenth, he was one of only a handful of people still alive.

But he had to be dreaming. Soon he would see goats wearing reading glasses or transparent hot-air balloons filled with marshmallow crème and that would be it for this nightmare. Goodbye, crazy-ass subconscious, hello six a.m. and the morning news on the NBC affiliate, Channel 12, with the pretty anchor talking about another homicide down in Gilpin Court or a dog attack on a petite widow out for a stroll with her Bichon frise puppy. The smell of coffee brewing in his coffeemaker. The hiss of the machine followed by the reassuring trickle into the carafe, the pungent aroma of coffee spreading through the house.

But the dream hadn't ended, it had kept right on keeping on, and he sat there, cocooned by the silence, its big brawny embrace squeezing him until he could barely breathe. Then he tried to force the dream's hand, thinking maybe he could declare a jihad against it. At noon on the twenty-first, he wandered out onto his porch wearing nothing but black dress socks and running shoes. Everything about it seemed wrong, and that was what he wanted, standing there with his wang and balls hanging free, he wanted it all to feel wrong because that was what usually pierced the heart of a dream. But there he was, in the big empty summer day, naked as the day he was born. When that didn't work, he jogged down the steps and headed east on Floyd Avenue. As he ran, he heard nothing but the sounds of his ragged, shallow breathing, the thrum of blood whooshing in his ears. On he ran, sweat slicking his body, and he began to cry, his sobs echoing off the houses of his dead neighbors. He ran faster and cried harder, and when he finished the loop around the block, he'd sat on his porch and cried like a baby. He went inside and hadn't been back out since.

Since then, he'd spent much of his time on the

couch with his laptop, drinking, eating peanut butter, watching Internet access grow spottier and spottier, the news channels go off the air one by one. One of the last news reports he'd seen was of a nuclear power station in Michigan melting down when the staff had failed to execute the plant's emergency shutdown procedures properly. It was like watching your favorite team get its ass kicked on national television. Except this time, the team was mankind.

Now he had a burning desire to be outside while there was still light. He cracked the front door, just a sliver, and when he was convinced it was safe, he stepped out onto the small concrete porch, his hand gripping the neck of the whisky bottle like a weapon. The air was thick and heavy, the feeling of wearing a sweatshirt on an unexpectedly warm fall day. He lit a cigarette right away, mainly because it made him feel tougher, because it made him feel like he had a grasp on things. You walk down a street and see a guy on his porch smoking a cigarette and drinking Jack from the bottle in the middle of the mother-fucking apocalypse, that is a guy you do not want to mess with, right?

The sounds of summer were huge and everywhere, the cicadas buzzing, the birds chirping. In the distance, he could hear a dog barking. The hum of the overhead power lines in there somewhere. But underneath that was a huge void of silence.

A flicker of movement to his left caught his eye,

and he looked over to see a cloud of flies buzzing around a body in his neighbor's yard. It was Jeannette, the poet, lying dead on her perfectly manicured lawn, the grass still a bright, resplendent green. Adam stared at her blankly, the way he might have looked at a painting he didn't quite understand. She was dressed in pajama pants but nothing else; her hair was a tangled mess, and her face was bloated, caked with blood and mucus. He wondered how she'd ended up in her yard, how long she had been out here. Had she crawled outside, sensing the end was near, unwilling to lie for all eternity in a hundred-year-old brownstone?

The scope of what happened crashed down on Adam like a rogue wave and stole his breath away. It was always there, lapping at the shores of his mind, but it was these big waves eroding his sanity like an unprotected sand dune. Had he not lived through it himself, he wouldn't have believed such a catastrophe was even possible, and he was a doctor, a full-fledged, card-carrying man of science. The speed at which the virus overwhelmed everything had been dizzying; it was as if the battle to contain the outbreak had been lost before it had even begun. It was a thousand, no, a million times worse than anything he'd ever imagined. And here he was, standing at the end of history.

A breeze rustled the trees, full and thick with summer foliage, the leaves whispering amid the dying light of the day. Thunder rumbled in the distance, a low guttural drum. Adam looked west and saw a line of black clouds moving in, flashes of lightning laced into them like strobe lighting. It had been dry in Richmond for days; he'd heard faraway thunder each of the past few nights, but the storms had swept around the city, doing their duty elsewhere. The approaching tempest riveted him for a bit, like the passage of time had, because a summer storm right now was exquisite and ordinary all at the same time.

A series of electronic chimes from behind him broke him from his trance, and at first, he thought he'd imagined it. Broken out of a daydream by another daydream. A sure sign of insanity. But a few moments later, he heard the chimes again; it was his iPhone, the sound drifting through the screen door. His goddamn iPhone was chirping inside the house. An e-mail. A text message. Someone had tried to contact him. Rachel. He flung the screen door open, his eyes desperately scanning the house as the door clacked shut behind him.

Where was it? Where was it? He closed his eyes and, a moment later, he remembered he'd dropped it in the basket on the little end table by the front door after one of his many efforts to reach her. He had tried calling, emailing, texting, he had sent her messages through Facebook and Twitter, but he didn't know if anything was getting out.

He brought up the home screen (noticing with

some alarm that he had less than a twenty percent charge) and saw the numeral 1 stamped over the telephone icon. After plugging the phone in to charge, he tapped the icon to enter the voicemail module, where he found a single message waiting for him.

Rachel's Cell

August 22

9:42 p.m.

August 22? That had been two days ago. But the message had just landed in his inbox, leading him to the conclusion that it had been hung up in the ether somewhere, and had just managed to make it through the once-impossibly clogged communications lines. Maybe they weren't clogged anymore because there wasn't anyone left to use them.

He tapped the screen again, activating the playback function. Outside, the wind freshened as the storm drew closer. A burst of static, and then:

"Dad?"

Her voice was an atomic blast of light in his darkening world.

"I got your messages," she continued. "All of them showed up on my phone at the same time. I've tried calling you like fifty times."

Adam felt his heart break, an almost palpable sensation of his chest caving in. His daughter needed him, and he hadn't been there. Every decision he'd made in his life since the day Rachel had been born had been just flat out wrong, because they'd added up to put him here, clear across the country from his daughter, where he couldn't do shit for her in her darkest hour of need.

Father of the Year!

"Jesus, I hope you get this," she said. "Mom's dead. Everyone's dead."

Her voice cracked and then she sobbed for a moment. Then she took two deep breaths before continuing. Adam didn't dare move a muscle, didn't even take a breath, lest he somehow fuck up and delete her message.

"It's the 22nd," she continued. "I think. I'm headed up to my stepdad's condo at Tahoe while I try to figure out what to do," she continued. "I'm not sick. I don't think I'm going to catch it. I don't know how. I was hoping it was hereditary. No, that doesn't make sense. Because Mom died. But maybe the immunity passed through you. I still feel fine. Is it bad there? I haven't seen any news in a couple days. But it's so bad here. So fucking bad. Sorry for the F bomb. Everyone is dead."

She was rambling now, and Adam could hear the panic in her voice. She broke down again, but it was softer this time, more measured, more controlled.

"God," she said, her voice trailing away. "I don't even know if you're alive. Please, if you get this, please, please call," she begged. "The power is out here, but I guess the cell towers are still running somehow because I'm still getting a strong signal. I'll leave the phone on as much as I can, charge it with a car adapter. I'll do that until the cell towers go down."

Adam heard the tinkling of glass breaking in the background of the call, and he froze. He waited for her to come back on the line.

But she didn't.

"End of messages," a mechanical female voice said.

Adam played the message again, tears streaming down his face as he listened to her voice a second time. He checked his watch, his trusty Casio, faithfully marking the passing time. If she was still symptom-free two days ago, that meant she'd almost certainly survived multiple exposures to the virus. As best as he could tell, the disease was winding down by then, certainly in any decent-sized population centers. He called her back immediately, but the line wouldn't connect.

Did she share his resistance to the disease? Was it hereditary somehow? Some recessive gene buried deep in the Fisher DNA that had protected them? He told himself to calm down, to look at it clinically, to not get his hopes up. Anything could've happened in the last two days. This set off a huge debate in his subconscious, one that he decided to ignore for the time being. Up front, he set himself to gathering more information, more data, more evidence as to what might have become of her.

He played the message a third time, scouring it for any clues that Rachel might have left about her experience. The power was out in California, not surprising given the energy problems the state had had even before all this. She sounded alone, a single flickering light in a dark and dying world. Heading for Tahoe wasn't the worst idea in the world. Safer than staying in a metro area, but the idea of her by herself out there made his throat tighten with panic.

He had to get to her. Nothing else mattered.

A boom of thunder shook the house, sending Adam's balls into his chest. He slammed the door behind him, locking it, and moved deeper into the house, away from the windows. He ran upstairs as the skies opened up and unleashed a monstrous deluge of rain on the city. The rain was deafening, louder than any storm he'd ever heard before, its sounds amplified, as if Mother Nature was sporting a bullhorn, making sure whomever was left was listening very carefully.

AS THE STORM RAGED OUTSIDE, he spread a large map of the continental United States out on his bed and plotted his course. Richmond was a bit of a gateway town, the nexus of three major interstates – I-95, I-64 and I-85. Whereas I-95 hugged the coastline from Maine to the tip of Florida, and I-85 plunged south into

Dixie, I-64 meandered away from the ocean, toward the plains. Interstate 85 was his best bet. Away from the mountains, but digging deep into the heartland before an eventual westward turn on I-40.

He packed slowly, taking his time, carefully going through each room in the house. He filled an emergency kit with medicine, bottled water, canned goods, matches, a rain poncho. Then he packed clothes, toiletries, flashlights, even the photograph of Rachel he kept by his nightstand. From the closet in his bedroom, he retrieved a handgun, a nine-millimeter Glock he'd owned for years, since medical school, when he'd lived in the slums near downtown. It was wrapped in a white hand towel. He thought back to his close call up the street with the man who'd tried to shoot him. The very thought of shooting a gun again made his heart throb, as if his chest were too small to contain it. He'd taken the Glock to the range a few times, but it had been a while. He made a note to fire off a few practice rounds when he was out on the road.

The basement he saved for last, where he got to work dusting off old, rarely used camping gear. The place was dim and dank, and he was glad he'd tucked a flashlight into his pocket. The bulb sizzled and popped when he flicked the switch, and so he worked by the light of the hall corridor upstairs, using the flashlight for pinpoint work. As he picked through the detritus littering his basement, he thought about the origin of his gear, a byproduct of the thing with Stephanie, the outdoorsy one.

She was a third-grade teacher at St. Catherine's School, a friend of a friend. She was nice enough, and they had some good times, but they'd never really clicked, not in the way that said forever. They'd hiked along the Appalachian Trail a few times, and she knew what she was doing, whereas he did not. He ended up buying a thousand bucks worth of camping gear and then decided he needed to break it off. She hadn't seemed all that upset about it. There hadn't been any tears or long talks or anything like that. He saw her out with another guy a few weeks later, and he briefly debated approaching the guy and offering to sell him the tent and the backpack and the GPS tracking device because when was he going to use any of that shit?

And then it hit him that Stephanie was probably dead, and this felt tremendously unfair to Adam, that he was standing here, preparing for the camping trip of a lifetime, and it was only because of Stephanie that he was properly equipped to take it on.

He lugged the tent and the backpack up to the main floor, trying and failing to envision the days and weeks ahead of him. There was no frame of reference for this. For as much as he knew about the world in its new form, he might as well have been dropped on the surface of Mars. But what choice did he have? He had to get to California, to Rachel, because finding her meant he was doing something. Because finding her meant he had some purpose left.

He thought about Patient A, for the first time in days, and it occurred to him that his case before the Board of Medicine had been continued, postponed indefinitely, postponed forever. Patient A was still dead, but, he supposed, so were the nine members of the Board of Medicine. He would never get to tell the story about what happened, clear his name, and then he felt guilty because how could he think about *Something Like That* in the face of *All This*.

The thoughts just kept whizzing by as he inventoried his supplies, and he couldn't stop them, like he was watching train after runaway train race by from a deserted subway platform. Patient A and Natalie, the office receptionist who, inexplicably, had hated Adam from the day he'd joined the practice and basketball practice and his high school basketball coach who had skipped town in the middle of his junior year of high school and losing his virginity to Dena Chamberlain while his dad was passed out on the sofa and his dad, Donald Fisher, his giant prick of a dad, who'd gotten off easy, preceding the rest of the world in death by five years, lucky enough to have gone out via a massive stroke. Little League and the free soda they got at the end of each game. The way they'd fill the cup with a little of each kind of soda, a suicide they'd called it. Going to birthday parties at Chuck E.

Cheese's and the feel of warm video game tokens in his hand.

The tears sluiced down his cheeks to the corners of his mouth, and he tasted salt. He wiped his eyes and his face, ran his hands through his hair, and then laughed at himself a little because just who the hell was he cleaning himself up for? He hadn't seen a living soul in days, and he wasn't entirely sure he hadn't hallucinated that little incident. He was looking out his window on the morning of the twenty-second when a man in full cycling gear had ridden by on Floyd, up out of the saddle, hunched over the handlebars like he was leading the peloton at the Tour de France. He raced by, never looking up at Adam, never slowing down as he zoomed west.

Another crash of thunder, this one rattling the windows, and the power died, the residue of the light hanging in the air like a ghostly apparition before it, too, faded away. The basement was plunged into black-ness, a darkness so extreme that Adam couldn't see his hand in front of his face. In the black silence, he could feel the blood rushing in his ears, the way the ocean sounded on a dark night.

You just need your eyes to adjust, just give it a minute.

But his eyes didn't adjust, and it remained pitch black, a photo negative, the inverse of light. It felt ten degrees hotter in the room, like someone had started preheating an oven; a drop of sweat traced its way down Adam's flank. He began seeing shadows rippling against the wall, even though he knew he was imagining it, twisted shadows of evil men whispering to each other and rubbing their bony hands in anticipation of a sleepy little boy drifting off, like the ones he had seen through his bedroom window as a child. A bug of panic crawled up his legs.

He bolted for the steps, crashing over a half-filled laundry basket on the way, and raced up the stairs as if he had escaped a portal from some hellish dimension. By the time he burst into the corridor on the first floor, he could barely breathe, the fear lassoing his airway like a cowboy roping a steer. He tried to collect his thoughts, to remind himself what he still needed to pack, but his box had ruptured like the bulkheads on Titanic, and now terror was flooding the hull of the H.M.S. Adam. He'd kept it in for two weeks, but that was over now; every strand of his DNA had sounded the alarm, the one you did not ignore.

He felt his way down the hallway from memory, and mercifully, his keys and phone were still in the basket where he'd left them. As he grabbed his keys, it hit him. His SUV wasn't here. It was still down at Holden Beach. He had no car. He giggled. He couldn't stop himself, and the giggles bloomed into full-blown hysterics. His laughs echoed in the evening gloom, bouncing through the ether, sounding huge and insane. Tears streamed down his cheeks.

Insane. You're going insane, he thought as the giggles faded away.

He grabbed a flashlight and went next door to Jeanette's, the rain soaking his clothes. Her Honda remained parked at the curb, and her body was still lying in the yard, *just another scene from the apocalypse, dontcha know?* Her body had been picked over some by the animals, which really must have been sporting giant woodies with the vast selection of carrion that had suddenly been bestowed upon them. Adam avoided looking at her as he went up to the front door and let himself inside.

The house was a wreck. Clothes, food, the sour stench of something turned over. He stepped gingerly to the kitchen, where he knew she kept her car keys, hoping they were still there. He found them on the counter and then he rushed back outside, down the porch steps, and back to his house before the hot spike of guilt overwhelmed him.

It's OK, he thought. It's an emergency.

He loaded the car as quickly as he could, oblivious to the storm raging around him. When he was done, he ran back inside to change out of his wet clothes. He had to go, go, go! But as he did so, standing there in his wet shorts dripping on his floor, the absurdity of his impatience struck him. Where was he going at this hour, a terrible thunderstorm buffeting the city, the power out? He suspected the going would be tough enough in broad daylight, but to try it now would be just asking for trouble. In the morning, he decided. He would set off in the morning.

By nine o'clock, the storm had pushed off to the east, leaving behind a clear, moonless night. Adam stepped outside to smoke a cigarette. The darkness was total and complete, the city sealed tight in black ink. Sure, Richmond had had its share of storm-related power outages, but those were usually brief, nothing like the immense blackness he now faced, as though the entire city had been shoved inside a body bag and forgotten. No generators hummed, no candles warmed the windows. That was the difference. Blackouts had once been communal affairs, bringing people onto their porches with their Pinot and gin and tonics, their cigarettes and their pipes, laughter peppering the evening air, their jam-packed schedules paused, if only for a little while. This, though, was something else. Unseen back rooms of impromptu parties, where the roaches and spiders and rats scurried about, where evil men lured small children and young women and left forever scars no one could see.

He spent the night on his couch, the gun perched on his chest.

He woke to clear skies and a cool breeze. The city was silent. He did not know what lay ahead, but he was glad to be alive.

After a meager breakfast consisting of a granola

bar, Adam loaded the trunk with the last few supplies and started the car. The engine was loud in the immense silence.

He took one last look at his house and pulled away from the curb into the great wide unknown.

TO BE CONTINUED IN...

VOID

Book 2 of The Immune Series

Read On for an Excerpt

PREVIEW OF VOID

THE IMMUNE BOOK 2

How lonely it is going to be now on the Yellow Brick Road.
RAY BOLGER
THE SCARECROW

ONE

Dawn.

The sun spread its virgin light across the plains, covering up the darkness like a fresh coat of paint. Miles Chadwick was up early, as he usually was, sipping coffee and looking out across the eight-hundred-acre Citadel compound. He kept his office in his living quarters, on the second floor of the main building. Floor-to-wall windows looked west toward the growing fields, which would provide sustenance for their new world, the proverbial bottle for the infant society. It had been a good summer for the crops, and the land was alive, breathing, pulsing. The summer harvest was in full swing, tomatoes, cucumbers, peppers, squash, zucchini coming into the kitchens by the truckload. A pair of tractors was already out, chugging along, preparing the ground for the fall planting season.

He still found it hard to believe they'd made it. They'd executed the plan to perfection. As he did every day, he thought about the first time he'd met Leon Gruber, the German billionaire who'd made all this possible. Gruber was the majority stakeholder in the Penumbra Corporation, a multinational conglomerate with nearly 100,000 employees worldwide. Penumbra had its fingers in a number of pies, most notably transportation, energy, weapons, technology, agriculture, and pharmaceuticals. Starting when he was twenty, Gruber had built the company from the ground up and held more than ninety percent of its shares.

When Gruber approached him, Chadwick had been in Special Pathogens at the Centers for Disease Control and Prevention, passed over for promotion yet again. Gruber approached him at a Wendy's near the CDC and invited him to head up his private lab, dedicated to the study of exotic pathogens. The lab was off the books, with no government oversight to interfere with their work. As he sat there, chewing his spicy chicken sandwich, Chadwick relished the idea of telling his bosses in Special Pathogens to go fuck themselves.

The facility was top notch, the security better than he'd seen at the Centers for Disease Control. He'd never asked where or how Gruber had assembled the Citadel's stock of pathogens, the viruses and bacteria that could lay waste to millions of people; he wasn't sure he wanted to know the answer. He worked there for six months before Gruber told him what he really wanted Chadwick to do.

It had been a good six months, the most productive in Chadwick's career. He was having dinner at Gruber's home on the lake in the northwest corner of the compound, briefing the elderly man on his work. Chadwick believed he was close to developing a vaccine for Ebola Sudan; it wasn't the deadliest of the Ebola strains, but a vaccine would constitute one of modern medicine's great achievements and would be worth billions for Gruber and Chadwick. A huge victory against the tropical viruses that kept health officials around the world awake at night and wondering when one would mutate just right, bust loose like the cartoon Tasmanian devil, and take humanity down with it.

At first, Chadwick thought it had been a hypothetical question.

Could he fashion a virus deadly enough and communicable enough to wipe out the human race?

Enjoying the academic nature of the conversation, Chadwick talked about the challenges inherent in such an endeavor. Balancing virulence with communicability, both of which would have to be at a level unseen in human history. Engineering it so that it wouldn't discriminate against this ethnic group or that age group. Possibly a virus that was constantly mutating so that the human immune system eventually gave out. It would be tough, Chadwick had said, but not impossible.

"So will you do it?" Gruber had asked.

At first, Miles had nearly choked on his meat, laughing. But as he wiped his lips with his napkin, he looked at Gruber and knew the man was most certainly not joking. He didn't know how he knew. He just knew.

In that moment, as the proposal hung there, pure, virginal, a Schrodinger's cat of an idea that had neither been accepted nor rejected, he expected to be filled with horror. But he hadn't been. Saying yes, joining the greatest conspiracy the world had ever known, had seemed so easy, as though he had been meant to do it.

"Yes," Chadwick had said.

"I realize what I'm asking you to do," Gruber said. "But don't think of it as me asking if you to end the world.

"Think of it as my asking you to end climate change.

"Hunger.

"Racism.

"War.

"And for Zoe," Chadwick had said softly, almost unaware that he'd said it. He was almost in a trance, picturing a world that he could control, a world stripped clean of all the evil that had cut its purity like cheap heroin.

"And all the Zoes," Gruber had said, placing his hand on Chadwick's shoulder. He hadn't even realized Gruber had gotten out of his chair, now looming above him. "It's time for the world to evolve, Miles."

Chadwick drank his scotch.

"You knew I'd say yes, didn't you?" he said to Gruber, unable to look the man in the eye.

"I couldn't afford not to know," Gruber said.

And so he had gone all in with Gruber.

Zoe.

Chadwick tried not to think about her because it had been better, less painful, to pack it away deep, rather than think about the meth-addled mugger who had shot his new bride Zoe, six months pregnant, right there at the ATM machine in Atlanta for the forty dollars she had just withdrawn. Twenty-eight years old, a brilliant career ahead of him, and just like that, his life had been turned into a smoking crater. Her killer had never been caught, and Miles took some small measure of comfort in the thought that the virus had almost certainly exacted justice for him and Zoe and their unborn baby. When you got right down to it, the virus had been for *him*.

So he'd worked and worked, creating iteration after iteration, each virus coming up a bit short until finally, he'd developed Medusa (although it hadn't been his name for the virus, he thought it was terribly apropos). Then the gathering of the test subjects, the runaways, the vagrants, the homeless, the ones who had already slipped through the cracks and wouldn't be missed. That last clinical trial was unlike anything he'd ever seen. Aerosol infection of Patient Zero, then exposing her to Patient One for less than *fifteen seconds*, then One to Two, a chain of exposures, and so on through Patient Forty-Four, the virus airborne and moving even before the host developed symptoms. The virus infected every single test subject, and within thirty-six hours of exposure, every single test subject was dead.

But left unchecked, the virus would be the villain of the story Gruber wanted to tell. No, their story needed a hero. And that was where James Rogers, a specialist in nanomedicine from one of Penumbra's subsidiaries, had come in. He used cutting-edge nanotechnology to build the vaccine, the yin to the virus' yang, the light to its dark. They'd been prouder of the vaccine than the virus, using technology to assert dominion over nature, these microscopic machines coded specifically to target and destroy the Medusa virus.

Telling Gruber about each project milestone, recruiting the team to the Citadel, planning the August release, which they had code-named Zero Day, it had all gone off without a hitch. Then about a year before Zero Day, Chadwick received word that Gruber, who was rarely at the compound, had died at the age of eighty-four. Penumbra's general counsel, a man named Dave Buckley, had shown up at the compound bearing the news. He told Chadwick that Gruber's will had bequeathed his privately held fortune to the Citadel entity and left specific instructions that the project was to continue unabated with Chadwick at the helm.

Keens in Manhattan, the night they'd released the virus at Yankee Stadium. After Miles had received the telephone call from Patrick Riccards, his director of security, he'd kept on drinking, the alcohol serving as a restrictor plate for his panic. He'd polished off most of the bottle of Dalwhinnie and woke up the next morning with an exquisite hangover. That afternoon, he caught a flight to Omaha, where he'd left a car, and drove three hours to the Citadel compound. The place had been his home for more than a decade, and he had worked hard to integrate himself with the nearby town of Beatrice, Nebraska, about twenty miles to the east. He was generous with his time and his money, he appeared in town frequently. He was a big believer in the hide-in-plain-sight theory. There was never any local curiosity as to what went on in the compound because people just liked him so damn much. He threw parties, organized toy drives. There was even an annual 5K race for charity. Well, there had been, at least.

He'd waited out the plague at the compound, even dropping into town once the virus popped up in that section of the state. He saw patients in the local emergency room in the first week of the outbreak, before things had just totally collapsed. Even he had been stunned by the pathogen's virulence; he felt close to madness as the dead piled up, in the hospital and urgent care clinic near the center of town, in the churches and houses, from the trailer parks in the southern part of town to the aging Victorian mansions in the east. Although he'd heard about the massive traffic jams in some of the big cities, that hadn't happened in Beatrice because these people had had nowhere else to go. Many of them had never crossed the town limits in their entire lives, rooted to their birthplaces by poverty, family, lack of education, lack of opportunity.

There were one hundred of them at the Citadel now, the chosen ones, handpicked by Chadwick himself. It had been a long, careful process, one that had taken years. None of the men were older than forty-five; the oldest woman was thirty-six. His and

Rogers' first recruit had been Charlie Gale, a psychiatrist who'd worked with NASA in screening candidates for a manned mission to Mars. Then the government had all but scrapped the space program, a decision that, as it turned out, had been one of the nails in humanity's coffin. A checkpoint on the highway to extinction. Chadwick had little use for a society that elected to stop learning, to stop exploring. The vast universe beyond the Earth's troposphere, a rich, undiscovered bed of mysteries, and mankind had said, *Nope, we're good!* Together, Rogers, Chadwick and Gale had developed the criteria for membership in the Citadel so they could identify those that would thrive in the new world they were creating. There was no room for error, none whatsoever. Each recruit had to be perfect.

Fifty men. Fifty women. They were doctors, engineers, scientists, botanists, agronomists, survivalists. Single and never married. No children. Rigorous physical examinations. No religious background or participation because the last thing he needed was for humanity's saviors to wipe each other out in a holy war six months later. Even more rigorous psychological evaluations, because these people had to hold up once they executed the plan.

And he didn't even put them through the Citadel screening process until he himself had performed his own thorough background check on each of them. He'd followed each of them for months, studied their habits, their trash, their comings and goings, read their Twitter feeds, subscribed to their public Facebook postings.

There had been hiccups, of course. One bright doctor, an epidemiologist who had looked terrific on paper, quickly figured out what the Citadel was up to. That was as close as the project had come to being exposed, and that was when Chadwick realized how lucky he was to have Patrick Riccards as his head of security. Riccards was ex-CIA, a former covert operative who'd served in Afghanistan. Riccards had sensed a vibe from the kid, nothing more than a hunch. But he'd sniffed him out.

The coffee contained a healthy splash of Bailey's, a little habit he'd picked during the first week of the epidemic, as they'd watched their dark dream come to life. As they watched global news coverage delivered via the satellite linkup, as they'd stayed in contact with their field operatives, his heart was constantly racing, racing, and he found the morning cocktail helped throttle things down a bit. He didn't know why he was so on edge, why he'd been snapping at his senior advisers, even after it became clear they'd executed the plan flawlessly, that the virus had exceeded their wildest expectations. Based on some of the field reports, mortality from Medusa had exceeded ninety-eight percent in many areas.

And the nanovaccine had worked perfectly. This

had been their greatest fear. That the vaccine would fail at the critical moment, that someone would break with the virus. But no one did. Three people had developed non-specific symptoms in the first week of the outbreak, incidents that had launched their collective testicles into their collective throats, but they hadn't become ill. One person had experienced a mild heart attack during the epidemic, revealing a previously undiagnosed heart condition, but he had recovered and was on medication.

It was all but over now, and it was time to look ahead. Time to begin the work that would carry him through the rest of his life. A quiet world, a blank canvas on which to paint his masterpiece. A new society in which the population was carefully controlled, in which the planet was given time to heal the scars inflicted upon it by the weighty load of seven billion people. But a world in which they'd have all the freedom they could ever want. A society free of crime, of fear, of hate, of partisanship, of ideology, of extremism, of wants, of hunger. They could recreate society in their image, in his image.

He was still considering his options regarding the unvaccinated survivors of the plague, the ones beyond these walls, the ones who, whether they knew it or not, whether they intended it or not, constituted the biggest threat to his grand vision. Chadwick estimated there were approximately five to seven million survivors in the United States alone. Not today, not next month, probably not even next year. But eventually, they could undo everything they had worked so hard to build. He'd put it off long enough. He had to spend some time coming up with a solution.

Five million survivors.

Taken out of context, the number was huge, overwhelming, the size of the Chinese Army, at least until about two weeks ago, but in truth, the number alone meant nothing. These survivors were scattered all over the place, virtually none of them would know each other, and many of those would go through another weeding out in the coming year, people who were in no position to survive the harsh reality without the modern conveniences they'd all come to depend on. As many as twenty-five percent of the survivors were under the age of eighteen. At least a million, possibly two million, wouldn't make it through the winter. And the North American landmass was enormous. Even before the epidemic, large swaths of the continent were unpopulated. These survivors were just pinpoints scattered across a blank canvas.

The rest of them, though, the ones Professor Darwin would be really impressed with, would become battle-hardened with time. They would adjust, evolve, possibly assemble into a threat, especially if they ever found out the truth about the Citadel. That was their greatest secret, the one that had to be guarded at all costs.

He drained his coffee and looked at his calendar. Chadwick had meetings this morning, meetings all day. There was so much to do, so much to keep track of. First up was Dr. James Rogers, who had been running tests on Citadel women in preparation for the project's second critical phase. Chadwick checked his watch and sighed. It was ten after six. He was already behind schedule. Rogers was due at six, and he was normally early to their meetings. As he waited, the day breaking clear and hot, he poured another cup of coffee, passing on the Bailey's this time.

Rogers knocked on the slightly ajar door just as Chadwick finished stirring in his sugar.

"Come!"

Rogers stepped in the room. The physician was pale, bleary-eyed, his clothes rumpled and disheveled. Highly unusual for the fastidious medical director of the Citadel. It was obvious he hadn't slept. Chadwick went in for a sip of his coffee, his eyes locked on Rogers' face, and ended up with a hefty gulp of the steaming liquid. He felt it scorch his tongue, and wasn't that just a hell of a way to kick off the day? All because he thought he'd seen something in Rogers' face.

"What is it?"

"You're going to want to sit down," Rogers said. He was a tall man, lean, his skin pale from years in the lab.

He kept his fine blond hair short, close to the scalp. He was a brilliant pathologist and a pill popper who'd had his license to practice medicine indefinitely suspended.

Chadwick noticed that Rogers had not apologized for his tardiness, which just made Miles even more nervous. He felt the ligaments in his knees loosen, and he nonchalantly grabbed the edge of his desk, lest he collapse from nerves in front of one of his closest advisers.

"What? Is it the virus? Is someone sick?"

"No," Rogers said. "No, it's not that."

He was silent for a moment, picking at his lower lip. He didn't make eye contact with Chadwick, focusing instead on something on Chadwick's desk. Miles followed his gaze to the commemorative baseball on the corner. It had been signed by each member of the St. Louis Cardinals team that had won the 2006 World Series. Looking at the ball twisted something inside him, and he remembered how much he would miss baseball.

"The test results are back," Rogers said. "We've discovered an anomaly."

"What anomaly?"

"In the female subjects," Rogers said.

Annoyance tickled Chadwick like a feather; he hated it when scientists spoke so robotically. Maybe if they'd been a little more approachable, a little more human, maybe none of this would have been neces-sary. Shortly before the outbreak, Chadwick had read that sixty-one percent of the American population didn't "believe" in evolution. As though it were some-thing you had to believe in. It was like saying you didn't believe that two plus two equaled four. He often wondered who was to blame for such a travesty. Had scientists done their jobs right, maybe the world wouldn't have needed this reboot, this reformatting of its hard drive.

"Jesus, what anomaly? Stop beating around the fucking bush."

Rogers folded his hands together and tapped the fist against his lips, like he didn't want to verbalize his next thought, lined up like a reluctant airplane waiting for takeoff.

Now Chadwick was pissed and scared; a ripple of heat shot up his back.

"We ran anti-mullerian hormone testing on all fifty females," Rogers said. He was still looking at the base-ball. "This test checks ovarian reserve."

"I know what it does," Chadwick said sharply.

Rogers ignored him.

"The results were disconcerting."

Chadwick spread out his hands in front of him, as if to say, "And?"

"In each of them, the AMH levels were virtually zero," Rogers said, finally looking up at his boss. "We ran additional tests, FSH in particular, and the results were the same. Complete ovarian failure."

Chadwick sat down and scratched an itch on his palm. That had meant something once, that money was headed your way, right? Good fortune? Well, that was a load of shit because Dr. James Rogers had just dropped an atom bomb in the middle of the Citadel. He felt a big, idiotic grin spreading across his face, and he felt his breath coming in ragged gasps.

"Ovarian failure," Chadwick said softly.

He thought about all the work they had done, the years of sacrifice, the careful, precise planning, and the idea that it had all been for nothing made his stomach flip.

And then, quite unnecessarily, Rogers added: "Miles, all of the women in the Citadel are infertile."

"How is that possible?" Chadwick asked. The question was partially rhetorical, as he already knew the answer. There were only two options.

Either the virus had sterilized the women.

Or the vaccine had.

Fifteen minutes later, Chadwick was in the main conference room with Rogers and his other three top advisers. Rogers and Patrick Riccards, the Citadel's director of security, were engaged in a heated discussion, on their feet, their faces red, like two baboons getting ready to tussle.

Margaret Baker, the director of operations, was in tears, something Chadwick immediately took note of. He wondered if he should cut her some slack. She was thirty-five and hoping to give birth to one of the first Citadel babies, and he could understand her despair. But could he trust such an emotional hair trigger of a woman? He'd never seen the slightest hint of emotion from her, not even a wisp of regret or empathy as Medusa had incinerated the human race. You just never knew with some people.

If the virus was to blame, and every surviving woman on the planet was now infertile, then none of this mattered. This was all window dressing, a really shitty after-party, and they were just the epilogue. Another few decades, and the sun would set on the human race permanently. The Earth would go back to doing whatever it was doing before *Homo sapiens* became the dominant life form, and Chadwick didn't think mother Earth would miss them all that much.

He preferred this scenario because then it meant it wasn't the other scenario. If it wasn't the virus (and he really didn't think it was), that meant it was the vaccine that had done this. Their vaccine. He'd almost been prouder of the vaccine than he'd been of the virus. It had been the ultimate exercise of dominion. In Medusa, he'd created the ultimate weapon, a mechanism to alter all things. But in the vaccine, they'd created something even greater.

If Medusa was the devil, Miles Chadwick had been its God.

And all things served God. Even His fallen angels.

Or so he'd thought.

"Quiet," he said. "Everyone sit down."

He waited while they each found their seats. He was pleased and a little relieved that they responded so quickly. They sat like obedient schoolchildren, their faces open and scared and hopeful all at the same time.

"Up until now, everything has gone to plan," he said. "Better than we imagined. But now we've got our first crisis. Our first real crisis."

He thought of something else to say, but he wasn't sure how it would play. His pulse slowed, like a racecar throttling down, and he thought it ironic that it had taken the end of everything to make him feel like he was in control.

"And, quite possibly, our last crisis," he said casually.

He saw smiles on their faces, even a chuckle from Rogers. The tension seeped out of the room like a deflating balloon. It worked. They wanted leadership, and he was giving it to them. He was in charge.

"We need to find out if the infertility is a side effect of the vaccine," Chadwick said. "We need to bring in an unvaccinated female survivor. And we need one yesterday."

He looked at Patrick, who was already nodding his head, taking notes.

"I've got a team in mind already," he said. "We'll move out in the morning."

"What if it's not a side effect of the vaccine?" Margaret Baker asked stupidly.

Chadwick sniffed, and then let out a slow breath. He reminded himself she wasn't a physician. Rogers, who had been sitting quietly, his head down, focused on his hands, spoke first.

"Then we're all fucked," he said.

ABOUT THE AUTHOR

David's first novel, *The Jackpot*, was a No.1 bestselling legal thriller. He is also the author of *The Immune*, *The Living*, *Anomaly*, and *The Nothing Men*.

His short comedy films about law and publishing have amassed more than 2.5 million hits on YouTube and have been featured on CNN, in *The Washington Post*, *The Huffington Post*, and *The Wall Street Journal*.

Visit him at his website or follow him on Facebook (David Kazzie, Author) and Twitter (@davidkazzie).

Made in the USA
Coppell, TX
11 August 2020